SWORD OF THE DEMON

SWORD OF

THE DEMON

A NOVEL BY
RICHARD A. LUPOFF

HARPER & ROW, PUBLISHERS
NEW YORK, HAGERSTOWN, SAN FRANCISCO, LONDON

FIRST EDITION

Designed by Patricia Dunbar

Library of Congress Cataloging in Publication Data

Lupoff, Richard A   1935–
    Sword of the demon
    I. Title.
PZ4.L9627Sw3   [PS3562.U6]   813'.5'4   76–5543
ISBN 0–06–012717–1

76 77 78 79 80 10 9 8 7 6 5 4 3 2 1

SWORD OF THE DEMON

I

The figure in yellow.

Beneath those feet: blackness.

In all directions: darkling void permeated with primal matter, nascent whirling atoms, free particles, proto-dust primed to coalesce through the action of incipient gravitation, ready for friction to generate radiation, hovering on the brink of heat, on the edge of night.

The figure in yellow: frozen in a timeless instant.

There is neither movement nor energy, sensation nor thought. The figure in yellow, hominoid, featureless, its face and body a continuous satiny surface. Its form, androgynous: small breasts, nipples erect, penis and scrotum visible through a thin membrane.

A free electron is attracted by the gargantuan gravity of a single proton. They approach each other. An energy flux flares into brief existence.

The figure in yellow turns slightly in the direction of the energy flux. Its posture is unaltered: there is no evidence of volition: a tropism.

The free electron and proton collide. There is a momentary broadcast of energy as the electrical charges of the particles cancel. A neutron survives the event. The figure in yellow quivers imperceptibly.

The figure in black.

The face of the figure in yellow turns. This is a change in the posture of the being. It directs what might be a glance at the figure in black. This being is wholly asexual, its flat chest devoid of paps, its crotch a plain curve, a simple concavity, glistening like satin.

The figure in black raises an arm, points one finger at the figure in yellow.

The figure in yellow turns to gaze toward its own hand. This is unformed, spatulate, ovoid. The figure stares. Undifferentiated protoplasm is shaped, articulated into digits. It clenches a fist, opens, spreads its fingers, looks again toward the figure in black. It duplicates the gesture of the figure in black, purposelessly pointing with a new forefinger.

The figure in black glares. A mouth opens in the satiny ebon face. A red-black clot of thunder emerges from lips like coal, rolls slowly forward, passes the pointed finger. A cruelly hooked talon curves from the tip of that finger.

The ball of thunder sails through the distances that separate the figure in black from that in yellow. The red and black thunder, moiling and pierced with discharges of electricity, crashes alongside the head of the figure in yellow. For a moment the cloud grows until it envelopes the head, then penetrates the yellow exterior.

It is the first sound heard.

The figure in yellow clutches its head in anguish. Its second hand, mitten-like, forms itself into fingers and thumb, bones and nails. It clutches its head. Its mouth falls open.

The first speech is a cry of pain.

It turns to flee. Bones and muscles work in its legs. It runs away.

The show has begun.

Beneath its feet distantly spaced particles are distributed through the blackness. It runs at first clumsily, irregularly. Its arms flail in imbalance. Its chest pains it, its head pounds, its ears ring.

Within its chest it feels a terrible pressure. Beneath the satiny yellow skin, undifferentiated protoplasm is becoming structured. It opens its mouth, gasps for breath to fill the new, empty, pain-drenched lungs. It draws breath.

It stumbles and sprawls among the nothingness, tumbling and skidding. The empty blackness offers no purchase to widespread feet, clutching fingers.

It fetches up against a clod of newly condensing matter. More massive than the tumbler, yet the lump of matter skitters slowly away, accruing additional particles as it glides through the void. The figure in yellow rebounds, collapses, is stationary, momentarily stunned.

It sits up, shakes its head, blinks its eyes, gazes back in the direction from which it has fled. All is blackness, blackness pointed with specks of unspecifiable color. One point glimmers faintly and moves, relative to the rest, at a barely perceptible rate.

The figure in yellow turns. Far now in the direction of its ended skid there is a radiant glare. Matter is accumulating, the clot that stopped the being's movement is itself flying, gathering additional particles, colliding with stray bits of substance, growing in dimension and accrued energy, beginning to glow, its rolling motion visible as a whirling and echoing of spiroid tracks made of dust and gas.

From behind the tumbler comes a roar. The figure in yellow turns to face once again the point of its own first appearance. Moving toward it is a speck of ebon glare against the background of darkness.

The figure in black.

The figure in yellow stands steadily, illumined from without and from within: the living androgyne. Her breasts heave with each straining breath. His genitals ache from the effort of flight.

The figure in black approaches, glistening darkly against the darkness, eyes glowing like embers, breath glowing like incandescent gas, crotch a smooth concavity.

It extends its two arms toward the androgyne. It strides forward. It nods. It almost smiles.

The figure in yellow watches its approach, eyes flickering

cat-yellow, hands at its sides. Her waist is gracefully slim, her hips curve gently outward, his pelvis supports his small phallus lightly.

The figure in black advances. It is close now.

It smiles.

The inside of its mouth glows as do coals, its tongue flicks once, red, gleaming, bifurcated. It hisses a breath at the other. Its breath is crimson, radiant with heat.

The figure in yellow quivers. It takes a step forward, toward the other, but then halts. They are still some distance apart.

The figure in black inclines its head in suggestion, in invitation.

The figure in yellow takes another half-step forward.

The figure in black hisses another breath toward the androgyne. The breath seethes with orange-red sparks.

The hand of the figure in yellow is extended. So close are they that the hand feels the red breath. The figure in yellow draws back its hand, presses it in pain against a satiny cheek. Tears brim in the tumbler's eyes.

The tumbler turns, draws away once again. The figure begins to run, more surely with this attempt, beginning with a great bound.

From behind, a taloned satiny-black claw sweeps downward. It catches the figure in yellow, catches the flesh of its back. The claws penetrate the skin, although not deeply. The figure in yellow pulls away. The claws rip downward, leaving ugly parallel scars.

There are two screams: from the figure in yellow, of fear and pain; from that in black, of rage frustrated.

The figure in yellow runs gracefully this time, firm legs better developed, *technic* improved by practice. Long strides cover great distances rapidly. There is no looking back.

The figure in black pursues. It lacks the developing grace of its prey: in its movements there is no beauty save that of dedicated function. Its legs move with machine-like regularity. Its exhalations are fiery. Its skin gleams a polished blue-black.

Beneath the feet of the two, blackness pounds back, jolting

each runner with every stride. From afar they are two specks, one of creamy yellow, one of burnished blue-black. Their eyes gleam: cat-yellow, ember-red. One figure moves with sexual grace, one with mechanical precision. Their pace is identical.

In the frigidity of the void their exhalations linger in the air behind them as each stride carries the runner past its own most recent spoor: yellow cloudlets, red cloudlets.

The back of the yellow runner aches. It is the claw tracks of the black's assault that cause the pain. A soreness begins to spread from the scratches just as it would had a local toxin coated the gleaming talons that dug those furrows.

The shoulder and arm of the yellow runner ache. The neck aches. The legs are as yet unaffected, yet the runner is becoming fatigued. The figure glances over its whole shoulder, sees its glittering black pursuer keeping pace. The price of this information is the loss of some small distance, perhaps half a pace, in their separation.

The figure in yellow begins to search for a place of refuge, an avenue of escape from that black pursuer.

The pursuer continues implacably onward. As its prey turns and searches for a home-free, the pursuer continues forward, its only sign of fatigue the ragged cadence of its breath. Each is an outburst of boiling cinders. The black mouth opens an ember-red. Black eyes glare crimson.

Before the yellow being open endless vistas of darkness. The primitive particles have gathered now into concentrations: specks, clots, lumps, blobs of matter. Overhead the figure sees a giant wheel of fire. Increasing its pace, the runner begins to rise toward the spinning concentration of substance.

The figure runs uphill, glancing beneath and behind itself at the pursuer in black. It paces steadily, its breath coming in red bursts, its skin shining blue-black, its naked chest gleaming smoothly, its waist and hips straight, its crotch genderless.

Before the yellow runner revolves the whirling fiery disk. Behind there paces the pursuer in black.

The androgyne leaps through the blackness, arms outstretched like delicate membranous wings. It is propelled upward by the force of its muscular legs, arched back paining.

The runner reaches the glowing, whirling disk and halts. The androgyne seizes its edges, and holding it shield-like before itself turns to confront its pursuer. The glowing disk covers the androgyne's breasts and membrane-covered genitalia.

The follower in black has covered the androgyne's trail, its piston-like pace devouring distance, matching the strides of its prey one for one, gaining a fraction at each deviation from the pace of the yellow's flight.

The black comes to a halt. It is directly beneath its prey. It stretches upward with one taloned paw but cannot reach the feet of the yellow creature. It rises to its toes and swings its arms but it cannot gain the height of the yellow.

It throws back its head and bellows, monstrous roars emerging visibly from its mouth and hurtling upward to fly past the figure in yellow, curving away to invisibility in the distance of the void, their sound echoing faintly until they are so distant they can be neither heard nor seen any longer.

The figure in yellow peers downward.

The figure in black crouches, gathering the strength of its machine-like smooth body, its powerful legs. It springs with all its strength, its body uncoiling as it does so, its arms extended above its head, its legs trailing beneath it, toes extended, talons of fore and hind limbs curving wickedly in search of any purchase.

The figure in yellow recoils.

The figure in black reaches the level of the other, catches with its foretalons, scratching and scrabbling until it crawls to a position before the yellow.

The black looks searchingly into the face of the other, its red-glowing eyes locked with those of cat-yellow.

Slowly it rises to all fours, twitching a long, massive tail that disappears after a single sinuous swipe. It takes a short pace forward on all fours, glaring upward into the face of the other. It emits a sound somewhere between a growl and a purr. The vibrations drift upward, reaching the ears of the yellow. This hears and responds with a facial movement. The sound drifts past the yellow head and away, tumbling lazily along a path that carries it slowly downward and is gone.

The black figure rises to its hind feet, its forepaws lengthen into hands, its hooked talons shorten into gleaming metallic nails. Its face is a satiny blue-black, its eyes glow red. It opens its mouth and the interior glows a hot crimson.

The black places one foot forward toward the yellow. The yellow draws back.

The black takes another step forward. The yellow raises the whirling disk a small distance, holding it as if it were a shield.

The black tilts its head slightly, as if in appeal. It extends its two hands forward, satiny blue-black palms upward, nails curving at fingertips. It makes a small sound.

The yellow again retreats, but only a very small distance. Cat eyes travel from the face of the black figure to its flat chest, its straight torso, its entreating hands.

The yellow lowers its shield slowly. Its back aches with a throbbing dullness. It peers intently into the face of the black.

This one steps forward. It is not quite the same height as the yellow, appearing from moment to moment the slightest bit shorter or taller than the other. The yellow eyes drop to the feet of the black. The feet are long-toed, taloned. The cat-yellow eyes travel slowly up the piston legs, rest momentarily at the genderless place of their joining, then continue upward to lock with the red eyes of the other.

The black figure opens its arms, its forelimbs ending in perfect hands, the nails curved and sharp-ended. It moves slowly forward. The yellow stands stationary, hands at its sides.

The black reaches forward. It places one hand on the breast of the yellow, fingertips pressing into the soft flesh, palm against the small rigid nipple. The other hand it places on the yellow translucent membrane covering the male genitalia of the androgyne.

As if charged with a seething energy beyond the power of its endurance, the androgyne recoils from the touch of the figure in black, but that neuter being strides forward, maintaining its grasp. The left hand of the black entity, clutching the small breast of the androgyne, is as frigid as the blackest and most distant void. The right hand, clutching the genitalia of the androgyne, is searingly hot.

The yellow writhes, her nipple sending a powerful shock through her breast. His roasting phallus responds to the heated grasp of the figure in black, growing tumescent even in the agony of the other's grip.

The yellow mouth opens, yellow shouts emerge and fall heavily, bounding and rolling across the plane from which the two figures have arisen. The yellow androgyne writhes away from the neuter black. The talons of the neuter pierce the membrane enclosing the genitalia of the androgyne. Thumb and nail of longest finger tear toward each other. The membrane is split. The organs of the androgyne are exposed; the claws of the neuter hold only dripping shreds of torn membrane.

Again the yellow writhes. Her breast slips away from the frigid grip of the neuter. She whirls and runs a short distance, hurls herself into space, drifts gently downward.

As she drifts she holds her injured parts. Her torn flesh pains her at back and shoulder. From the burst membrane of his crotch a small blob of mucous egg-yellow fluid rolls along one thigh. He floats slowly, as if buoyed near to equilibrium. He rolls slowly, drifting downward, eyes turned back toward the height from which he had leaped.

Above, as on a promontory, the black figure stands, skin glistening bluely, eyes and mouth open, a ruddy triad of dim light. The yellow sees the swirling disk lying beside the black. The black bends, heavily raises the spiral in both its hands.

Limbs straining with effort, the neuter raises the disk above itself. It whirls the disk faster and faster above its head. Bright specks fly from the edges of the disk, elongated arms stretch longer yet. The black squats, rises, whirls, heaves the disk after the yellow.

The yellow begins to flee, drops her feet to the level plane, pounds away from the height. The whirling disk approaches closer and closer, emitting a piercing scream as it dances through space toward the yellow androgyne. Even as she runs she realizes that she cannot distance the whirling disk and instead swerves to one side.

She hears the disk whiz past her as she dodges.

She halts and turns to gaze after the disk. It skims rapidly, its axis parallel to the plane of the androgyne's flight from the neuter. She stands gasping for breath.

Back on the promontory, the neuter black watches angrily. It climbs slowly down, painful clawhold following clawhold until it arrives within a short distance of the lower plane, then drops softly to all fours. On padded paws it stands, neck arched downward, keen nostrils sniffing for the spoor of the androgyne. Its black tail lashes in fury.

Raising its head again, nostrils quivering, red eyes burning through the blackness that separates it from the yellow, the black entity starts forward, breaking quickly into a space-consuming trot. From time to time it drops its snout to the darkness beneath its feet, confirming the continued presence of spoor. From time to time it raises its head to peer crimson into the darkness ahead of it.

Its tail is long, heavy, restless. It has no genitals.

The androgyne, peering back into the darkness, sees the angry red glow of the beast's eyes. When the beast drops its head the glow disappears. When it raises its head the glare is renewed, terrible.

The figure in yellow prepares to resume its flight. For a moment he hunkers down, elbows on knees, forehead resting on crossed forearms, breathing raggedly. A spasm grips his intestines and suddenly he adds involuntarily to the spoor.

He rises, takes a few hesitant steps forward, stumbles, rights himself, and attempts a trot. He staggers badly, halts, gathers his failing strength. He stares behind him into the darkness. Twin dots of fiery hue peer after him. A larger, third glow appears beneath them. A cloud of milling hot sparks emerges.

The cloud roars forward, growing as it advances. By the time it reaches the figure in yellow it is larger than he is. It passes over and around him as liquid flows over a sharp rock. As it reaches his ears he hears it as a roar of hatred and impending triumph from the beast that follows.

The androgyne limps away from his pursuer. He stumbles over a clot of material, grasps it in his arms. It is heavy, dense, massive. The androgyne gathers handfuls of undifferentiated stuff from all around her. She begins to pound them onto the clot.

She does not permit it to grow larger, but packs it more densely, making it smaller in volume even as it grows in mass.

Its substance grows so great that increasing amounts of matter are drawn to it. The androgyne herself struggles to keep from being drawn to her own creation, plastered flat across its surface. She pulls in great armloads of flowing, rushing matter, pounding it with all her strength into the sides of the massive clot.

Streaks of matter now rush toward it from all directions. The androgyne can no longer resist the immense force. She looks about herself once more. She sees the figure in black, upright, hominoid, sexless, rushing as it too is drawn toward the huge mass.

The androgyne relaxes as she slips down into the deep heart of the mass. There is a sense of rushing, of pounding, of bursting, of transfiguration; there is an experience of the total lack of sensory stimulation.

Yellow cat eyes blink.

She stands, whole, on a dank cement flooring. Behind her, a massive metallic door, ajar. Ahead of her, a sight at which she blinks yellow cat eyes.

2

The cold beneath her feet is different from that of the plain
across which she had run. A solid coldness, textured, surfaced,
dank; gray mottled darkly by splotches of moisture: it is
ordinary. Barefooted, she strides forward. The damp floor
extends only a short distance, then she stands upon a different
surface.

A moist atmosphere presses hotly upon her skin. She stands
amidst streaming greenery. She is wholly female now: hair flows
across her shoulders, her breasts yield softly to the caress of a
warm breeze; her waist is narrow, hips broad, curled female
escutcheon arrows from soft belly to tender pubes.

Turning her head from side to side, she moves forward
slowly, blades of scrub grass massaging her insteps with each
pace.

The breeze that lifts her hair momentarily carries with it
sounds: the hum of varied insects, the swish of heavy fronds, a
distant sound of flowing water.

She looks up. The sky is like blue crystal. The sun is huge and
yellow-white. Slitted irises in yellow eyes narrow to bar its glare.
On her skin the rays of the sun are a tangible presence, pleasant
and welcome.

Other sounds reach her. They are deep, vague, like
monstrous crashings and boomings carried from a great
distance. Nothing nearby in any direction, she turns to gaze

back toward the doorway and naked flooring. She cannot find them.

Behind her a green plain stretches far: misted hills rise to meet the horizon. Ahead and to one side more hills climb jaggedly into the untainted blue, giving way to tall stands of vegetation and to the glimmer of rippling water.

She tastes the air, its flavors pressing on her tongue: brown-warm, green-moist, alive. She swallows. Her saliva carries the flavors of the air.

Nectar.

Her exhalations are at first characterless.

She paces toward green forest. Her feet toughen quickly. Calluses are unharmed by saw-edged blades of tough grasses. Her hands are empty. Her hair trails behind her. The sun beats upon her shoulders. Her back is smooth, soon beginning to tan to an even brownness.

There is only the suggestion of parallel lines running from shoulder to waist, a redness that may soon disappear beneath the brown that ripples with each swing of arm, each stride of leg.

She increases her gait to an easy trot.

She breathes easily, deeply, mouth open to savor the rich air, an undefined chant rising from her chest. A light flow of perspiration springs to her face, her chest, and her back. Droplets run down her legs, shaken and falling to the green plants with each strike of foot upon earth.

She feels the light jolt of each stride running from foot to hip, the play of muscles in her legs as each is raised, shoved ahead, allowed to drop back to earth. Her weight is thrown forward through long, easy strides, resting momentarily upon this foot, upon that foot. Her arms swing easily as she runs. Her breathing is strong.

Small shrubs begin to dot the grass-covered plain. Low, thick-boled, sturdy. As long as they are sparsely positioned she plots her course among them easily. The sun has slid from its zenith: it is afternoon. The warmth of the day has increased, her perspiration has grown heavier, the air within her lungs is also heavier, moist, tinctured with the suggestion of life.

A point glitters darkly near the earth, glinting featurelessly. It hovers for a moment, then darts through the air, seemingly disappearing into the dark green fronds of a low-standing, thick-bodied plant.

Transfixed, she halts.

Between two squat primitive trees a web glitters and bobs in the moist breeze. Its strands are thick, heavy, drooping nearly to the ground with their own weight. Its pattern is simple, radial strands interwoven with concentric polyhedrons.

In its center squats a fat spider, black and dull, covered with rough hair. It is as large in body as would be a cross section of a woman's leg taken halfway between knee and thigh.

The flash, the woman sees now, was that of a large flying insect, membranous-winged, captured now in the spider's web. Other insects flit through the heavy air. Some hover near the large spider. The spider does not move. The only movement in the web is that of the newly trapped flyer striving frantically to work its way free. Its struggles slowly grow feeble.

The woman resumes her movement across the plain. She too moves more slowly now. She is not obsessed with any fear of becoming entrapped, but cautiously she observes the spaces between the thick, short trees before passing between any two.

The trees begin to grow more closely spaced and in greater variety. Some are as tall as the woman, some taller. She perceives that she is entering the forest toward which she had been striding. As taller and more numerous trees are encountered, the areas of shade that they cast become larger and are less often broken by patches of direct sunlight.

The woman steps into a clearing. The ground is still warm here but it is cooler than had been that on the plain. The woman raises her face to the sky, cat-yellow eyes irising narrowly. Jewel-green tints of light arrow earthward where sunlight is caught in the accidental momentary focus of dark leaves.

The sun is falling. Already it is low in the sky.

From a tree limb a pair of eyes observe the woman. She

shifts her gaze away from the yellow-white sun. For the moment a complementary afterimage obscures her vision. Through this darkly glowing orb she perceives two tiny specks observing her. As she watches, the triangle is completed by the opening of a maw beneath the eyes.

A sound emerges from the maw, a startling shriek. For a moment the myriad noises of the forest, low and unobtrusive, are halted. A shocked stillness fills the glade, echoes from the woods surrounding it.

The woman makes her response to the shriek, a hardly formed vocalization, unarticulated. Briefly the glowing eyes snap shut. Only the open mouth remains. Then again one speck gives way to two. The humming of an insect emerges from within the woods. The sounds of life resume.

The woman shudders in sudden cold shadow. With her hands she rubs her chilled shoulders and upper arms. She draws a breath deeply, feels its lessened warmth, exhales again.

Turning in the direction of the water she had earlier seen, she moves off among tall trees. As she passes from the glade there is a soft sound behind her, a plop as of some soft-bodied creature dropping carefully from a frond limb to the ground. She looks back but sees nothing.

She walks beneath creaking trees. Their branches arch high, their leaves block the declining sunlight from the forest. The ground is covered with a layer of fallen vegetation, moist and cooling, soft beneath the feet of the woman.

There are soft sounds also. Scutterings from shadowy spaces near the trunks of trees. Gentle scrapings and slitherings from the branches. Everywhere, humming and buzzing, ever soft, ever quiet, ever present.

The wind must still be active, for the branches above waver and sigh. At the level of the earth, all is still.

The woman feels hunger. She looks at the plant life around her in search of something edible. She sees nothing of promise. She moves on.

Her body begins to send signs of fatigue. Muscles loosened

by sun warmth and exercise begin slowly to tighten and ache with the slower movement of walking in the cool shadow.

Deeper in the woods the woman hears the burble and splash of running water. She changes the direction of her march toward the sound.

She continues beneath the tall trees. Few smaller plants grow between their trunks. Where a rare break in the forest roof permits the entrance of sunlight there are grasses and bushes. Some of the bushes bear berries.

The woman stops before one such. She cocks her head toward the sky: the sun is nearly gone, the canopy's early evening colors changing from a crisp blue to a dark violet laced with flashings of gold, orange, purple.

She pulls a single berry from the bush. It is the size of the last joint of her smallest finger. Its surface is a dark red, formed with globular nodules. She holds it gingerly between forefinger and thumb, rolling it from side to side, placing pressure lightly upon it. A droplet of juice is forced from the berry and spreads upon her fingers.

She stares at the juice curiously, then raises her hand to taste it. She parts her teeth. Her tongue licks the berry's juice from her fingers, leaving a thin track of saliva on the skin of her hand. The juice of the berry is tart and warm. She pops the berry into her mouth and chews it slowly, the juice and pulp sampled by tongue, teeth, cheeks, the roof of her mouth. The tartness makes her grimace but she decides that the sensation is not wholly unpleasant.

She plucks a large bunch of berries from the bush, holding them in both her hands. She places a few in her mouth, chews and swallows them pleasurably, eats more, sits on the cool vegetation with her legs crossed, her hair thrown back, eating happily until all the berries are consumed.

Red juice paints her tongue and lips, dribbles from her chin and runs between her breasts, accumulates momentarily in her navel, then runs again to disappear into the shrubbery between her thighs.

When she has finished eating the red fruit she licks juice from her hands, wipes them on her body, rises, and moves again in the direction of water.

As she does so, a dark shape scuttles from beneath the berry bush and disappears between two thick-boled trees.

The woman feels the chilling evening air on her body as she walks upon soft, cool vegetation. The sound of water is closer. She attempts to see through the trees and the evening gloom. Cat eyes widen with effort.

Unexpectedly there is a break in the woods. Before the woman stretches a narrow beach; beyond it, water.

She stands beneath a tall tree. Before her, pale sand gleams weakly in the last light of dusk. Wavelets foam softly against the shore, reflecting light impinging from the horizon. The water's surface flashes irregularly with the ripples and small splashes of its flow.

Beyond the waves is another narrow strand, and beyond this lies land of a nature unlike that of the forest.

The woman steps from between dark, drooping trees. There is a scuttling noise from behind her. She crosses the sand, feeling in it a remnant of the day's warmth, its coarse grains adhering to her naked feet.

At the edge of the water she squats momentarily, searching the woods behind her for pursuit, then falls to her belly and drinks, lapping the water with her berry-stained tongue. It is icily chilling yet fresh and pleasant on her face and in her mouth.

Thirst slaked, she rises. Where red juice had streaked her body, now there is a rough coating of sand. She brushes at it, then stops and walks forward to the water.

Marine arachnids and water beetles scuttling about on the surface scramble to avoid the woman, save one arthropod, fat-bodied, black, red eyes aglow. It squats perilously, its weight distributed in an octagonal pattern upon the surface of the bearing liquid.

It watches the woman, neither advancing nor withdrawing from her presence. The woman fixes the creature with a yellow glare. Its mouth opens and shuts. The woman walks beyond it, the water growing deeper as she proceeds. She turns and moves in the direction of the flow of the water.

By the time she is beyond sight of the fat arachnid the water has reached her thighs. She gasps: a sudden, deep inhalation; and plunges into the water. It envelopes her flesh coldly. She whirls in its embrace, rises to the surface with her face to the sky, hair floating about her on the water. She scrubs sand and red juice from her skin, the juice carried away from her body by cold flowing water, the sand sinking slowly in large granules to the bed of the river.

She dives beneath the surface of the water, examines the clear depths and rocky bottom with eye and hand, rises and breaks surface. She feels a sudden hot pain at the base of her neck, drops again beneath the edge of air, paddles fearfully, resurfaces. Behind her she sees a large black wad struggling frantically on its back, legs thrashing the air. Two or three red spots glow amidst the black as the creature struggles.

The woman feels the river bottom beneath her feet. She staggers through shallows, emerges from the stream onto a grassy bank.

On all fours she drags herself around to search the water with her eyes. One or more red glowing spots, their number uncertain, seem to disappear beneath the surface of the water.

The woman crawls away from the water's edge, finds a bush covered with oddly shaped leaves, their apparent color nearly black in the onrushing gloom of evening. She plucks a handful of leaves with fingers growing stiff and numb. She presses the leaves to the painful place on the back of her neck.

She stretches full length upon the grassy ground and lies with her face to the clear sky. In its blackness she watches countless stars standing in perfection against the unmarred void.

A moon rises from behind treetops and leaves. It is huge, pale.

The woman sleeps.

When she awakens it is to the touch of a hand on her flesh, the sight of a face above her own. The stranger is taller than she, or would be, she judges, were they to stand side by side.

She does not move, but cat-yellow eyes observe.

The stranger is black of hair, his touch strong. The woman cannot see much of the stranger's face, but she can see that he is smooth-shaven, bending to care for her.

He places a hand beneath her shoulder, another on her side, and turns her so that she lies prone upon the grass. Carefully he removes the leaves from the wound on her neck, rises, and walks away. When he returns, the woman observes that unlike herself he is not naked.

Black cloth covers his body; his loins are wrapped in a dark linen garment-like trousers, a *dhoti;* a shawl on his shoulders is draped to fall in graceful curved folds, black piped with white, flashed with scarlet. From his shoulder hangs a scarlet pouch. He removes it, places it on the ground beside the woman, and kneels. He opens the pouch and draws from it something that he presses against the wound on her neck.

He speaks as he does so, but the woman is chiefly aware of the feeling in her wound. For an instant its throbbing ache is intensified into searing pain, then a soothing warmth replaces the flame. The soreness and nearly paralytic stiffness that she had felt give way to a tingling sense of relaxation. She turns upon the grass and rises to a sitting position.

The stranger, too, has arisen. He stands face to the sky.

For the first time since awakening, the woman is aware of her surroundings. She can hear the water flowing. She can see its surface faintly by the dancing lights it reflects from the sky.

The sky itself is still dark, star-patterned. The moon has set, the woods from which she had come are still. The air barely stirs.

Farther up the bank from her the land grows higher, its features lost in gloom. The water itself flows onward, making soft sounds to itself as it moves. She scans its surface for any glowing red dots, but there are none to be seen.

The stranger is still standing with his face upraised.

The woman stands, walks to his side. Her body feels light to her, comfortable. Her head is slightly giddy. She pauses beside the stranger and places her hand upon his arm. The arm is thinly fleshed, its bones surprisingly vivid and unpleasant to the touch. She pulls her hand away.

The stranger turns to face her. His forehead is startlingly broad for a face otherwise so narrow, his cheeks almost painfully lean, his long hair emphasizing the verticality of his features. She explores the depth of his dark eyes, seeing there the suggestion of some other-hued glitter.

The man takes the woman's wrists in his hard, nearly fleshless hands and draws her to stand before him instead of at his side. He holds her thus, uncomfortable, facing him.

He speaks to her.

She gazes into his face and shrugs.

He repeats his words.

She indicates again her incomprehension.

He speaks in other words, different-sounding words, a complex jargon of vowels and stops replacing the growling gutturals of his first speech.

Still she does not understand. She shrugs helplessly. A sudden chill passes through her body, making her shudder.

The man removes the shining black cloth from about his bony shoulders and holds it toward her. She slips it around her own, softer shoulders, feeling weak and slightly nauseous. She tries to say something to the man, very nearly falls but instead feels herself supported by his bony hands.

She feels herself being half led, half dragged by the man along the stream's bank.

As the man and woman move beside the water she feels the texture of his garment against her skin. Its finish is rough, its friction against her body restores chill-impeded circulation to her arms, her shoulders, her breasts.

Stumbling along, half asleep, she feels herself halted. She looks around. The sky is lightening along one horizon, streamers of yellow and orange pierce the heavens. The black dome of night fades into a pre-dawn shade of grayish blue.

She is still held upright by the man. Again he speaks to her and again she is unable to comprehend his speech.

He points ahead.

She follows the direction of his motion and beholds a great beast standing on the stream bank, grazing.

Cat eyes open in amazement, irising wide. The size of the creature is greater than she can comprehend. Its shape is astounding, its color incredible.

The man leaves her side; she finds herself able to stand unaided. The man walks to the side of the beast. He strokes its snout, the beast having raised its head at their approach.

The beast gazes at the woman. The man speaks to the beast. The woman is unable to hear the man's words.

The beast kneels.

The man returns to the woman. He still wears the black *dhoti* piped in white, flashed in scarlet. In the growing light the woman sees that his nude torso is painfully thin, his skin extremely pale; for an instant she hallucinates a stark vision of his bones, his very organs working beneath that thin, translucent flesh.

He gestures peremptorily at the woman, then at the beast. She walks to a place beside the creature. The man takes her hands and places them on either side of the gigantic head.

He speaks to the beast. It presses its face against the woman's body. She receives from it an impression of immense power.

The man leads her to the other side of the beast and assists her in mounting.

The man climbs upon the creature, taking a position before the woman.

The beast carries them away. At its first steps there is a squelching sound. The woman looks down and observes a black clot mashed into the earth.

Swiftly the creature rises from the ground.

3

The beast is ridden saddleless, its waist long enough to easily accommodate two riders, narrow enough to be sat comfortably astride. Its strength is such that it seems not to notice the weight of the woman and the man.

It springs forward, legs carrying it lightly off the ground. From behind its frontmost shoulders it raises large translucent wings structured with semirigid veins. In the growing light of morning these brilliant wings diffract the new sun's rays into shimmering spectra.

The creature rises into the air, its head arched forward, wings beating rapidly. As it increases its speed and rises into cooler layers, a rushing slipstream whips the long hair of the woman behind her. She can feel it snap against the small of her back, her spine and shoulders, like tiny lashes. She gasps with pleasure, gulping mouthfuls of sparkling, chilled air.

The man is seated before her, naked to the waist. His back is hard, bony, and pale, sinewy muscles moving visibly as he presses and prods the beast between his and the woman's knees. The woman can see the head of the beast and the world ahead of them by raising her eyes to look over the man's shoulder. Seized by sudden impulse, she thrusts her hands beneath the man's arms to hold tight to his chest; she can feel his ribs singly through his thin flesh.

The man signals to the beast with his hands. At once it dips, head thrust forward, wings flush against its sides. Beneath them the woman can see the flowing water beside which she had lain. Here its course has broadened and deepened; the sandy bottom cannot be seen from above. A thick growth of trees surrounds it closely, fronds and limbs overhanging shaded banks.

The beast, diving vertically, carries its riders swiftly downward. The woman sees broad-leaved trees grow larger as they descend. For an instant their mount again spreads its wings, its progress slowing. The woman holds her position by clamping her knees and ankles against the sides of the beast.

The water beneath them seems to be frozen in flickering timelessness, the sun and unclouded sky reflected flawlessly in its smooth surface. The woman can see the reflected face of the beast: large, faceted eyes, bulging cranium, prehensile proboscis. Its wings are a blur even in this wink of vision. Its legs are tucked against its belly; the woman cannot count them.

The face of the man is visible in the water mirror, rapt in concentration on the flight of the beast. The woman sees her own hands, her feet, her face peering downward.

Water plumes up, making icy white spray blossoms in the shape of lilies. The sound of their impact smites the woman's ears. The chill and shock of sudden frigid immersion crash onto every point of her skin.

She holds tightly to the skeletal man before her and the creature between her legs. In the last possible instant before the water embraces her she gasps her fill of morning air. As the beast and its riders submerge, the mount extends its wings and its legs, using them variously for propulsion and the direction of its course.

It settles into a path angling gently downward. The woman, holding her breath, peers straight down. Shafts of sunlight penetrate the clear water far into its depths before fading away, but the bottom cannot be seen.

The man half turns, twisting at the waist to face the woman.

Her air is short, pressure hard within her chest, a ringing in her ears.

The man exhales conspicuously, his exhausted breath rising in glimmering bubbles from his open mouth and from his nostrils. He inhales water.

The woman, nearing panic, looses her grasp on him and the beast. Before she can pull away and rise toward the daylight above them, the man twists farther and grasps her wrist in his bony hand.

Her breath explodes upward, bubbling from involuntarily opened lips. Unwillingly she draws chill water into her throat. Its savor is surprisingly pleasant. It fills her lungs. She does not choke or gag. Amazed, she exhales. A few tiny bubbles trickle upward.

The man releases her. He gestures, inviting her to resume her place on their mount. He pulls her back to her former place behind himself. She regrips the beast with her legs.

The creature continues downward. The man and woman on its back breathe the water comfortably.

The woman's ears hiss and ring with pressure. She swallows water and gains relief. The water is utterly clear. Through it she hears sounds faint and remote. As of distant trumpets, distant timbales.

She tries to ask her companion the source of these sounds, whether they are real. She finds that the movement of her mouth is slowed and mildly impeded by the water, but that she is able with little effort to speak.

Is there music?

The man turns to present his face to her. He replies in a voice that slashes clearly through the water, in yet a third tongue, but still she recognizes none of his words, takes none of the meaning of his speech.

She shrugs, puzzled.

He turns away.

The beast carries them steadily deeper into the water. The clarity of the medium is such that the rays of the sun penetrate deeply, deeply. Yet, as they continue, strangely breathing, the sound of distant music hovering at the edge of their hearing, darkness grows about them.

Darkness grows.

The water is frigid.

The sound of the music is faint.

The woman is drowsy. The man faces ahead. The woman holds to the beast with her knees, to the man's bony form with her arms. She leans her head against his narrow back.

She is in complete darkness. The water is terribly cold. She can see as little with her eyes open as with them closed. The beast swims onward. The woman is unable to identify the direction of their movement from that of their entry into the water.

She initiates a question: Are we—? And stops.

The man looks back at her, this much she can tell from the feel of his body as he turns. But he does not speak: to what purpose would that be? He turns away. She feels the play of his muscles. He is communicating with the beast through sensitive areas beneath its now-folded wings. The rush of water about them increases.

Their surroundings are as yet lightless. The sound of the instruments may be present, so faint that the woman cannot tell certainly whether she hears them at all.

She strains her eyes against the darkness. Ahead of her by the shortest of spans she is able to detect the back of the man, knobby vertebrae ridging his thin, pale skin.

There is some light, then.

Using a pale arm, which the woman can now faintly discern in the dark water, the man raises his hand and points in a direction ahead of the beast and, by some trick of perspective, above its head. The woman perceives what may be a source of faint light.

They continue onward, their mount swimming upward in long, slow spirals. The woman and the man breathe the water that bears them. The light ahead grows by imperceptible degrees. The woman cocks her head in concentration, to one side, to the other. She cannot hear music. She wonders whether she has heard music.

With a shock the beast and its riders break through a surface.

They are surrounded suddenly by air. The beast floats briefly, then begins smoothly to swim.

The sky is full of night.

The woman expels lungsful of water: it runs from her hair and her body. She gasps at the sparsity of air when she draws it into her throat. It is flimsy stuff, thin when one has become accustomed to breathing water.

For some time she works to hold herself steady against giddiness at the thin atmosphere as she reaccustoms herself to breathing air. When her lungs are once more calm she turns her attention to scanning the skies. Millions of stars burn coldly green, purple, red, gold against the dead background of night. A huge moon hangs low at the horizon.

Silhouetted against it the woman sees a ship, prow high and ornately carved, sails furled, oars shipped. The sound of wavelets lapping against the gunwales of the ship carries across the water. She can hear it in counterpoint to the soft paddling of her mount.

The man before her nods in the direction of the ship. He prods their beast and it sets off paddling steadily across the water to the vessel.

The ship is long and graceful, clearly visible against the huge moon. Lanterns dot its decks and superstructure; tall masts and rigging hanging in shallow curves stand in black relief against the creamy brightness behind.

Raising his hands to his mouth, the man on the beast halloos the ship ahead of them. A cry echoes from high in the rigging of the ship.

The beast swims more swiftly forward, the water churning to luminosity beneath its powerful limbs. The ship looms higher and higher as the swimmer and its two passengers approach. When the hull of the craft crashes over them the beast swings broadside to the ship and paddles slowly toward her prow. It stops..

The man gestures to a rope net hanging from the side of the ship. As he does so he grasps a heavy cord with one hand and pulls himself from the creature's back, hanging on to the ropes.

The woman follows in kind.

Together they begin, climbing steadily up the side of the ship. As they near the railing the woman's attention is arrested by a great splashing from below. She turns her eyes to see the creature that has carried her and the man thrashing its way across the surface of the sea. Its wings are extended and flapping, its legs working rapidly against the surface of the water.

It rises clumsily into the air, dripping and shaking itself as it flies.

At the top of a long curve it levels its course and arrows away from them at amazing speed, disappearing into the distance of night even as the woman follows its course with her yellow cat eyes.

The woman turns again and hauls herself over the railing and onto the planked deck of the ship. The man has arrived ahead of her, clearly unconcerned with the behavior of the creature that has borne him here. He stands, waiting for the woman to join him.

Now he sets off, as obviously expecting her to follow as he had expected the beast to settle its own destiny.

The woman does not follow.

The man disappears amidst rigging and accouterments.

The woman walks about. Groups of sailors sit or stand, conversing quietly. They look up as she passes, then return to their own affairs.

A pale glow bursts from within a darkened cabin. The woman walks toward the source of light. A portal stands open, leading to a sound-and-light baffle. Carefully the woman threads her way through.

Inside, the cabin is dark. Its walls are hung with rich cloth of many shades: maroon, gold, ocher. The floor is soft and as warm as flesh, carpeted with some substance unfamiliar to the woman's bare feet.

From the ceiling, suspended by light chains, hangs an ornate pannier of burnished metal and carven wood formed into a miniature jewel-encrusted throne. Upon this an infant is seated, clothed in regal robes.

The room is dimly lighted by a glow that emanates from the child seated on the throne.

As the woman enters the cabin, the eyes of the child follow her with a cold intelligence far beyond that of an infant. She walks once around the cabin, satisfying herself that it holds no other inhabitant.

The infant does not move its limbs. In a thin, reed-like voice it addresses the woman.

She is uncertain of the child's language, but its meaning echoes within her mind with a clarity and cold force like that of a harsh hail ricocheting off barren rocks.

The infant demands of the woman her identity and purpose aboard the ship.

She makes a gesture, hands held before her chest, fingers upward, palms toward the infant. She moves her hands outward from her chest and away from each other, then drops them before her thighs.

She says simply that she cannot answer.

The infant half reclines in its strange hammock, contemplating her with eyes of cold emerald. At length it tells her to sit, so that they may explore the possibilities that lie before them.

The woman complies. She drops to the floor of the cabin and adopts a posture with legs folded, arms at rest, hands held in her lap with their fingers interlaced, palms upward.

The infant indicates approval, nodding carefully. Its voice is low in volume, thin yet authoritative. It speaks with the intonation of one who has lived a long life and a difficult one. The infant pipes to the woman that her garment is wet and urges her, for her comfort, to remove it.

The woman doffs her borrowed shawl, finding the cabin warm and dry after her long submersion in chilly waters.

The child says, softly, that the two of them can now know each other. If the woman does not know her own essence, the infant at least will identify himself to her.

He is the Miroku, the infant says, bearer of salvation to the land of Tsunu. When he is prepared to assume his true nature and person, then shall the ship make land at the gates of Tsunu and then shall he leave this ship *Ofuna*. He shall march in triumph to his vacant palace. Then shall he bring terror to his enemies.

The land of eternal snow and darkness shall know sunlight and lush grass. The ice shall give up its ancient secrets. Wisdom and the rightful power of the Miroku shall be restored— although the person known may be other than the person seen.

The beasts of fire shall leave the people and shall return to their lairs in the mountains.

There shall be feasting and celebration. The people shall rejoice. So it shall be in the land of Tsunu when the Miroku returns to claim that which is his.

The infant lapses into silence.

The ship leans to one side, creaking. The infant sways precariously on his throne. His eyes gleam emerald-green.

The woman feels the sway of the ship in her body. She asks the infant, When will this be?

When he is ready, the infant replies.

The woman asks how long he has been as he now is.

The infant has been on board *Ofuna* for some six score thousands of days, he tells her.

The woman's eyes, cat-like, open wide as she calculates the length of time.

For that long, yes, whispers the infant.

And when will he be ready to land at Tsunu, the woman asks.

The infant ignores the query. Instead, he asks in his thin, reedy voice, if the woman does not know her name, can she tell him other things. Whence came she? How did she reach the ship *Ofuna?*

The woman draws a breath, deeply. Hands in her lap, she speaks. There was—blackness. Blackness and cold. She and another, she tells, yellow and black. She was not then a woman, nor yet a man, but somehow both.

The other would have destroyed her, she tells the Miroku. It too was neither woman nor man, but as she was then both, the black one was neither. A mere thing, without sex.

Neither had any name, at least that she can remember. Only, the other sought her destruction. She fled. It pursued. She came, somehow, to a different place. A place with trees and grass, mountains, sky, sun, water. And living things.

And the man who brought her to the ship, riding upon the back of a great beast through deep waters.

The infant stops her with a gesture of one hand. What man brought her to *Ofuna,* he demands.

A man who— The woman hesitates. A man who found her near the woods, lying wounded by the venom of a great spider. He salved her wound, she recounts, carried her to a great beast that swam through deep, clear water and brought her here.

Deep waters, repeats the infant. Did she see the land at the bottom of the water, he demands.

The woman says that she saw no bottom. Only clear water growing darker as they penetrated deeper, then full darkness, and then they were rising once more.

They began in morning light, she says. When they rose from the waters it was dark night. The man brought her to the ship.

And now? asks the infant Miroku. Where is this man now?

Somewhere on the ship, the woman surmises.

One more question, woman, pipes the infant. As you passed through the waters, did you hear any sound?

The woman is uncertain of how to reply. After a silence she says only that she does not know.

Music? asks the Miroku.

The woman says she was never certain. Perhaps music. Perhaps music of drumming and of high distant horns.

There is no perhaps, the Miroku pipes. You heard. You are the sent one.

Now the woman is questioner. The sent one? What is the Miroku's meaning?

The Miroku pipes that he knows who the sent one is. He

knows also who is the man who brought her on the beast, to *Ofuna*. That one would not have willed to bring the sent one; he had not the choice to make.

The infant draws a breath that is nearly a sigh. To the woman, for an instant, the softly rounded face of the child takes on an aspect of a wizened ancient—but for an instant only.

Then the infant speaks once again. That one is his foe and hers as well. He would destroy them both if he could. But he was compelled to bring her to *Ofuna* once he had found her. And the mark of him is on her.

Behold yourself, Miroku commands.

The woman gazes at her body. Where the shawl of the man had rested on her shoulders, where the piping of white and flashing of crimson had lain, she is marked.

The infant speaks. You must know who you are, and you must know what is your purpose in this place. Listen to me.

You are the Kishimo, the sent one. It is to aid me that you are sent. Together you and I, the Miroku and the Kishimo, shall struggle to regain the land of Tsunu.

He who brought you here is the Aizen. He is a god as well as a man. You will learn more of him. For now, know that he is our foe. If he conquers, never shall the land of Tsunu know the rule of Miroku, nor shall the great events foretold come to pass.

But if we overcome the Aizen, you and I, then shall those great days come.

The woman says then that she is puzzled. Is the Aizen truly her enemy, and the Miroku's? And is he near them, on board *Ofuna*?

The Aizen is the chief of our enemies, the infant pipes. His powers can call demons and ghosts against us. His whereabouts can be known—he is surely on board *Ofuna* and in time they will surely feel his presence.

But now, Miroku suggests, they should strengthen themselves for the struggle with nourishment and rest.

4

Kishimo, then, is her name. Her hair is black, coarse, and long. Her skin is the shade of a faded olive, her body is strongly muscled, her face is smooth. Her eyes are yellow and slitted like a cat's.

She rests on her heels on the carpeted floor; there are no cushions or platforms for sitting in the cabin of the Miroku.

Retainers bring food.

The cabin grows warm with the heat of a small charcoal brazier upon which the food is made ready. Kishimo removes the shawl of the Aizen, taken once from her shoulders and then replaced there; now she folds it carefully, lays it aside, and sits anew, crosslegged, warm, as careless of her nakedness as are the others in the cabin.

When the food is prepared the retainers withdraw.

The Miroku, no larger than a common cat, rises from his place and descends by a small chain ladder to take a bowl. He fills it carefully and returns to his place without speech.

Kishimo, unmoving, follows with cat-yellow eyes. When the Miroku nods to her she rises, takes bowl and sticks, fills the bowl with food, and returns to her own place. In silence they eat.

The retainers enter once more and remove debris.

There has been no speech.

Now the Miroku questions Kishimo once more, asking if she can recall her origin, her history, her purpose. Kishimo is unable to do this. At length Miroku ceases to prod. It is useless, he admits.

The cabin grows darker; Kishimo sees no means for this darkening that has taken place.

Rest now, commands the Miroku.

The cabin is very dark, very warm.

Kishimo fetches the shawl of the Aizen and spreads it upon the carpeted floor. She lies silently upon it, drawing half of the cloth over herself. The charcoal removed by Miroku's retainers, the cabin begins to grow chilly. A single shudder passes through the body of Kishimo and she clutches the shawl more tightly, using its roughness to warm and comfort her body.

There is nothing to be seen in the darkness of the cabin, but sounds penetrate the baffle, creep through the timbers, seep between planks, hide beneath the soft sighs and hisses of breathing to spring surprisingly into silences between.

A distant tap, soft and brief, as of a small soft-wood mallet striking a peg into a channel.

A brief ringing as of hard metal upon fine crystal, the metal impinging with such delicacy that the sound given off is like a shimmering film of pastel colors.

There is a sound of trumpets, remote and silvery, soprano harmonies fading slowly to the point of inaudibility.

There is the sound of remote drumming, the shrill yammering of the snare, the trembling boom of the contrabass quivering into the rolling thunder of another reality.

Kishimo sees an earlier self, a different self, fleeing from another being through inchoate realms, pursued by roiling clouds of crimson and black thunder; she feels her back pierced and torn by angry talons, sees glowing scarlet eyes against jet, and quickly opens her mouth.

To scream?

To defy?

To plead?

The vision fades away before she learns her purpose. The pursuer shimmers and dissipates. She herself trembles and twists upright, fighting the shawl of the Aizen away from herself. Its length has curled about her throat. Her struggles have knotted and tightened it until her skin is raw and her breathing harsh.

She straightens the shawl, rises, drawing it about her shoulders.

The infant Miroku reclines serenely in his place. Kishimo gazes at him and notices for the first time the badges that the infant holds. In one hand is a gleaming jewel. In the other, a bright sword with hammer-headed blade and gilded copper mountings.

Miroku fixes Kishimo with his gaze. Kishimo must go out from this place, the infant tells her. She shall be fitted and then she shall go out.

Kishimo rises.

Miroku directs her to wait while he again summons his retainers.

They enter and fit her with clothing: kimono, breeches, slippers, decorated gloves that reach nearly to her elbows. About her brows, holding her long hair back from her face, a *han-buri;* the brow guard is carefully knotted.

She receives no weapons.

So quickly that they seem nearly to disappear like dream-visitants rather than to depart as in truth they do, the retainers take their leave.

Now go, the infant Miroku commands.

And what of the Tsunu people? Kishimo asks.

As they shall be, Miroku croons, but the Kishimo must make her own way first.

Kishimo bows her head, her eyes fixed on the jewel and the bright-bladed sword of Miroku. Raising her head, Kishimo turns, takes in hand the shawl of the Aizen and places it around her shoulders, covering her kimono.

She moves to the baffle, threads her way from the cabin of the Miroku. As she departs from the presence of the Miroku she is alert to any parting word but receives none.

She emerges from the baffle to find herself in a damp

companionway, its planking polished and lacquered with battle scenes in black and crimson and gold. Cat-yellow eyes adjust to dim illumination.

Kishimo moves softly and gracefully along the companionway. Panels and corridors open darkly from it but she continues to the end, climbs a flight of steep wooden risers, and emerges from the lower quarters of *Ofuna* onto the deck.

Masts rise about her, sails boom and wood creaks, the wind cries shrilly in the lines of the ship *Ofuna.*

Kishimo is spun by the force of the wind, its cold, wet fingers plunging through her kimono and light breeches to prod her body like harsh icy claws. Kishimo forces herself to turn about once more, to face what must be the prow of the ship *Ofuna.* The wind screams at her, the water tumbling along the hull of the ship roars its anger.

Clutching herself, Kishimo leans into the wind and strides forward. Great gray flakes of mushy sleet tumble from the sky. The light of the sun is spread across the heavens so evenly that no part of the sky is more bright than another, so faintly that Kishimo can look directly at any point above the faint horizon without narrowing her eyelids.

Sleet crusting her hair and brows, plastering her face, she passes working sailors like pearly wraiths crouching, bending, tugging at lines. The plunge of *Ofuna* through pounding seas throws sheets of spume into the air. It sweeps across the deck of *Ofuna,* spatters Kishimo like blobs of frigid mush.

She reaches the foot of another flight of risers and stands gazing upward. She sees a figure outlined against the gloomy clouds that whirl and jolt past *Ofuna.* She grasps a railing and hauls herself upward, approaching the quarterdeck. As she reaches the deck, a gust of wind hurls a fresh sheet of foaming brine at her; she staggers, holds firm, stands facing the man.

He is the Aizen.

He is garbed in light armor: *keiko,* or cuirass, of plated metal cross-laced with flame-red silk braid, the color vivid against the gray of the sky, the sea, the falling sleet; *hoshi-kabuto,* or knobbed helmet, laced also with flame-red silk braid, its *shikoro,* neckguard, rounded, laced in flame-red, studded with *hoshi,* metal stars.

He wears doeskin *yugake,* decorated gloves, similar to those placed on Kishimo's hands by the retainers of Miroku; those worn by the Aizen are marked with stylized *hoshi,* like his helmet. He is armed only with *daisho,* the paired swords, the long *tachi* and short dirk, or *tanto,* each in a lacquered scabbard thrust through his waistband.

His back is to Kishimo as she approaches him. He scans the sea ahead of *Ofuna* as she approaches, yet turns at her movement. How can he have known of her presence? No sound of footfall could emerge through the sound of the storm: wind, sea, and ship herself creaking and moaning while her lines scream against the chill air. Yet the Aizen turns and glares at Kishimo.

She is a tall woman, taller than most of the crewmen she has passed on *Ofuna*'s deck, yet the Aizen is taller than she by a hand. She thinks: As we rode the great beast from another realm to this, Aizen seemed thin and fleshless. Now he appears mighty.

Is it his *keiko,* his armor?

Or is the Aizen in fact altered in this realm?

The Kishimo extends a gloved hand, prepared to give thanks to the Aizen for his aid in the other realm. She recalls the statement of the infant Miroku: that he and she, Miroku and Kishimo, are the foes of the Aizen. That the Aizen is both man and god.

And yet—the Aizen had assisted Kishimo when she had been stung by the spider. He had brought her to *Ofuna.*

At his glare she drops her eyes briefly. Through the kimono plastered to her by freezing sleet she is suddenly aware of her body, her heavy breasts, nipples sensitive and rigid from cold, the dark escutcheon visible through brine-drenched cloth.

Kishimo raises her eyes. She sees that Aizen too has been gazing at her body.

The Aizen asks: You have seen Miroku?

Kishimo has.

You have spoken?

She nods.

And now, the Aizen demands—and now?

Now I— Kishimo hesitates. She does not know her own wishes. She does not know the nature of the man-god Aizen. She asks him: Are you the rival of the infant Miroku? Are you he who keeps the Miroku as he is?

The Aizen affirms that this is so.

Then you are the enemy of the infant Miroku, Kishimo continues. How can the infant Miroku remain comfortably below while you are above, commanding the ship *Ofuna?*

The Aizen grins unpleasantly. He gestures to Kishimo, silently urging her to advance and stand beside him. He himself turns away, looking toward the prow of *Ofuna,* awaiting the obedience of the woman Kishimo.

The wind continues to scream through the shrouds and lines of the ship *Ofuna;* the howling spume falls mostly upon the deck where sailors strain and heave, little of it dropping onto the quarterdeck where Aizen and Kishimo stand.

Kishimo makes her steps forward to stand beside the Aizen; her eyes are level with the lower part of his face. She sees him gesture once more toward the prow of *Ofuna* and beyond, to the dim and heaving waters that lie beyond the ship and that surround her groaning hull.

At last Aizen speaks. The wind howls, sheets boom overhead, tall seas crash, yet the voice of the Aizen penetrates clearly to Kishimo. The voice is deep, clear, powerful. The Aizen and the Miroku are united by no bond of friendship, he tells Kishimo. Their rivalry is old and on occasion bitter. Their intentions for the land of Tsunu are at odds.

But behold the Sea of Mists! commands Aizen.

He sweeps both doeskin-gloved hands to the horizon. A tall cresting sea breaks upon the bow of *Ofuna,* sweeping across her decks. The water foams and coils like a hungry monster. The gray of the sea is transformed to foam of a pale white and a sickly green that catch the even light of the sky and glow angrily.

Again the Aizen commands: Behold the Sea of Mists! His voice is louder than it had been, its timbre more vibrantly compelling. And yet again:

Behold the Sea of Mists!

The banks of roiling gray that rest on the heaving waters seem to respond to Aizen's words and to his gestures. Swirls and pillars rise to dance and flow across the surface of the waters. As the prow of *Ofuna* dips nearly into the green-gray foaming sea, the mists hurl themselves upon the ship's wooden deck.

The prow rises once more, shipped water races downslope, making for the dark and unseen stern of *Ofuna*. The gray shards and walls of fog, bodies of mist that settled so quickly onto the planking, are lifted with the rising bow. They sweep and swirl across the lower decks of *Ofuna*. Before Kishimo's eyes, sailors disappear into the gray swirls, then re-emerge as the fog moves along. Now the sailors look puzzled, stunned, pale. As if they had been swept by the fan of death.

A vagrant column of mist rises before Kishimo. The sails boom overhead and the ship heaves forward through the sea. The mist sweeps across the quarterdeck, approaching Kishimo with the speed of a racing stallion. Before it reaches her she peers into its depths. She sees forms within, gesturing hands and *tachi*, swords.

The mists envelop Kishimo and Aizen beside her; so thick is the swirling grayness that Kishimo, turning, cannot discern the man-god. She raises one hand and puts it forth: it encounters something very cold, very moist, that seems to cling to her palm, wrap itself about her wrist, creep along her forearm coldly, wetly.

Kishimo tries to draw away from the wetness but in an instant the body of mist sweeps away from the quarterdeck, rejoining the banks of fog that surround *Ofuna* and cover the water through which she plows.

Kishimo studies her hand. It seems unaffected by its brush with the creature of the mist, yet Kishimo feels as if she has herself come within a finger's breadth of some terrible doom.

She turns again toward the Aizen. In the gray light, increased now by the passing of the mist from the quarterdeck, his eyes appear brighter than before. They seem to glow with a dark flame, glistening like black lacquer specked with tiny points of red.

Now, grinning, Aizen speaks.

Should I and Miroku struggle for *Ofuna,* surely would the ship founder. The Sea of Mists would claim ship, leaders, and crew, without care. The *kappa,* water-sprites who dwell here, would welcome us to their kingdom. The *kappa*—or worse.

Aizen thumps his hands upon a wooden railing that marks the boundaries of the quarterdeck, lest the unwary, blinded by fog and spray, step over its edge. Thus do Miroku and I leave *tachi* and *tanto* in sheath; there will be time for longsword and armor-piercing dirk before the fate of the land of Tsunu is settled. Thus do our retainers leave longbow and arrow, *naginata* spear and *tanko* armor, stowed. When we have survived the Sea of Mists, then will the Aizen and the Miroku settle their differences.

Kishimo indicates satisfaction.

Turning to face her, his countenance framed by helmet, neck guard, and cuirass, the Aizen says: You will come with me. You will come belowdecks with me and see *Ofuna.*

I have been belowdecks, Kishimo replies. I have seen the quarters of the Miroku, beheld his light, eaten his food, been served by his retainers.

The Aizen throws back his head and roars. His thumbs are hooked in his waist sash. He throws open his mouth and howls with mirth. The sleet, still falling steadily from the grayness above *Ofuna,* lands whitely, softly, on the face of the Aizen. Kishimo sees tracks of moisture make their way from the eye of the Aizen to the tip of his chin.

You have seen the cabin of the Miroku! Aizen laughs. You have seen the retainers of the Miroku!

He reaches and takes Kishimo's upper arm in the fingers of his doeskin glove decorated with *hoshi* stars.

To Kishimo the sensation is overwhelming. When she had

ridden with Aizen upon the great beast, he had seemed a man of skeletal make. Before, when he had laved her spider's wound, he had seemed ordinary, kindly, strong.

Now in his grip her arm feels as though it has been seized in pincer of iron. She cannot tell whether the iron is icy cold or searing with flame. She knows that the Aizen could close his hand and crush her arm like a hollow egg between those iron fingers, but he merely steers her forward, to the fore end of the quarterdeck, to an opening in the railing that surrounds the deck.

She raises her eyes for a final glimpse of gray sky, dim mists, heaving waves of white froth, black and green and gray seas. The bow of *Ofuna* dips below the cap of a wave, the water hisses and teems across the planks, across the feet of Kishimo and Aizen, soaking their already drenched breeches to the shins, then slides away across the gleaming planks of *Ofuna*'s deck.

Sailors like gray *haniwa* figurines clutch railings or lines to keep from being swept away from the ship.

The Aizen halts Kishimo with a sudden pressure on her arm. His own metallic armor clattering as he does so, Aizen kneels upon the deck. While Kishimo watches, his doeskin-gloved fingers find a black iron ring sunk into the planking and swamped with cold black glittering water. He pries the ring upward until it stands upright upon the planking. He grasps the ring with both his gloved hands and, armor creaking even through the roar and whine of the storm, strains and heaves until the trap creaks open in the deck of *Ofuna*.

Kishimo responds to Aizen's gesture and clambers into the trap. Behind her she sees him flatten the ring once more in its sink-hole. Kishimo scrambles down a flight of wooden risers, Aizen following close behind. The trap is drawn shut with a deep and echoing thump. The sounds of the storm are muted; the clatter and hiss of sleet striking the trap, blended with the constant rush of waters along the hull of *Ofuna*, the roar and scream of the wind—all grow faint.

The trap now closed, Kishimo finds herself for a moment in

seemingly total darkness, but quickly her cat-yellow eyes iris wide to reveal a dim light flickering from below, bathing Kishimo and Aizen in feeble waves of illumination.

Kishimo sees Aizen pointing imperiously downward. She turns and sees the flight stretching far, far down. Can *Ofuna*'s lower decks, even her holds, descend so far beneath the level of open planking? Cat eyes blink, blink. The irises are opened wide. The light from below is far away.

Descend! commands the Aizen.

Kishimo places a slippered foot before her on the next riser of the flight. She moves to another, to another. Always close above her, the Aizen keeps pace. The deck and planking above them grow dark, faint to Kishimo's rare glances back. Soon all is black above. There is only the flight, darkness and Aizen above her, dim flickering light and risers dropping away, away, away below.

Kishimo descends. Here there is no railing for the hand at either side of the risers. The flight is easily wide enough to accommodate her careful stride; still she shudders at the sight of the risers' ends: beyond, the darkness falls away seemingly without end.

Halting, Kishimo turns with the purpose of asking the Aizen—something.

Before the woman Kishimo is able to speak, the Aizen gestures imperiously: a clenched *hoshi*-glove, a doeskin-covered finger extended: downward.

Kishimo turns back and continues. With each stride she is conscious of the danger of falling. The risers seem perilously narrow even though her eyes perceive that they are of the same width as ever. Each stride threatens to hurl her from the side of the flight to plunge silently, endlessly, downward.

Silently.

Her ears detect only the sounds of movement, her own slippers connecting carefully with each flat riser, the soft swishing sound of her kimono and breeches, gradually drying now, and the hissing of her breath. The sounds of the Aizen: his flame-red silk-bound armor creaking with each step, his *kogake* foot armor clanking with each stride, his own breath pumping in and out more slowly and more heavily than that of the Kishimo.

And again, through the soft sounds of movement, Kishimo hears or almost hears the low sounds of distant trumpets, distant voices, distant drums.

The light before her flares.

5

Iridescent blue, glowing the color of moth's wings.

The color flares; Kishimo sees no shape, no object by the sudden brightening except the color splashed across her own breast, arms, legs. Her body senses heat as well as light through her thin, brine-damp kimono until the flare drops away once more. But now the faint, distant light is stronger than it had been.

Kishimo continues carefully, pace by pace, until she detects remote rocky walls fitfully lighted by the incandescence from below. Rocky walls, rough and dark, the walls of an ancient cavern carved out by long-dead fires or long-dried streams. The illumination is brighter than ever but no more steady.

At last Kishimo sees a speck of distant blue. Far ahead, far below. She steps, steps, approaching the fire. Now she can see an end to the flight: a plain stretching away from the final riser, rocky and dead, and across the plain a blue flare flickers and dances on the rock.

She does not turn to inquire of the Aizen. Let him speak if he will. Kishimo continues ahead. Finally she breaks her steady stride, drops a slippered foot from the flat, polished wood to the cold, smooth stone. How many slippers have walked here, across how many years, so to wear away this dead rock?

Kishimo feels the hand of Aizen once again closing about her arm. This time his fingers pinch her forearm. She halts and faces the other, watching the blue-tinted face with its dark, glittering eyes and hair as black and coarse as her own beneath the bowl-shaped helmet. For the first time she sees the decorative motif of the helmet: a dragon flanked by twin thunderbolts.

Are we still within *Ofuna?* Kishimo asks bluntly.

The Aizen's reply is indirect: We will cross to the pit of flame. There we will find my retainers awaiting us.

Kishimo asks if the retainers of the Aizen were not the sailors who crewed *Ofuna* through the storm in the Sea of Mists.

The Aizen throws back his head in another of his frightful laughs. Sailors! He sneers. Sailors!

He releases his grip on the arm of the Kishimo, places his palm heavily on her shoulder, and turns her to face him. With his free hand he pulls aside her kimono, inspects her body. Satisfied, he removes his hands from her person and commands: Come!

He moves away from her.

Angered at his handling, yet the Kishimo follows. The plain they cross seems endless in extent; neither walls nor boundaries nor sky are visible. Kishimo finds increasingly that she cannot reconcile the existence of this place with the notion of being belowdecks on the ship *Ofuna.*

Perhaps this is yet another realm of being.

The flaring incandescence is ahead of her, ringing the Aizen with an aura of ultramarine as he strides ahead of Kishimo, between her and the flames themselves. Closer and closer they draw, and the flames grow brighter with each stride. Now Kishimo moves so that the Aizen is no longer between her and the flames, but ahead and to her flank.

She can see the blue, flaring as tall as three men mounted upon one another's shoulders. It rises from an orifice in the dead rock, the rock that gives back a dull remnant of the brilliant light fitfully splashing and raving upon its face.

The rock stretches beyond the source of the blue flare; at first it seems that the flame is the sole source of illumination in the cavern, but now Kishimo, straining her eyes to see far into the distance, recognizes tiny specks of identical blue brilliance dancing and flickering, and beyond them the suggestion of woods and of waters, of gnarled branches and leaves faintly illuminated by the flickering azure flame, the waters glinting so feebly that she cannot be certain that she sees these things.

Finally Kishimo and the Aizen approach the nearest and most brilliant of the flames. As they draw near, Kishimo sees figures surrounding the flame and hears a low murmur. She turns to see the response of the Aizen, but he continues to stride toward the flame, his armor clashing with each stride as lamellar plates slide and clatter and as his foot armor strikes the cold naked rock.

At last they halt at the outer ring of the beings surrounding the flame. At this close range Kishimo sees that the figures are squat, terrible, animal-like beings with wild hair and great teeth. They are armed with spears of many types: serrated-blade *su-yari,* curved *naginata,* lance-like *naga-suyari,* cruciform *jumonji-yari.* Others carry longbows and quivers of arrows with heads of iron pierced in the form of cherry blossoms or the eyes of boars.

Aizen approaches the demons and hails them fiercely.

The beings spring up, their energy remarkable: from their posture, squatting in circles about the shaft of ultramarine fire, they leap into the air, whirling and drawing weapons before they return to the rock. Dozens of them crouch and shamble, forming a crude half circle, their backs to the flames, their terrible figures now black in silhouette against the bright blue flare, facing the Aizen and the woman Kishimo.

The leader of the demons, so marked by three peacock feathers mounted on his *kabuto,* iron helmet, leaps forward once more. He plants himself before the Aizen, feet widely spread, glares briefly at the taller man-god. Kishimo watches, wonder filling her. The demon places both hands on the hilt of his curved *naginata* spear, then bows deeply to the Aizen and to the Kishimo; they return his courtesy; he leads them toward his people, whose ranks divide, making an opening for them. The Kishimo, the Aizen, and the chief of the demons make their way through this gap and squat near the rock fissure whence the blue flame flares.

The blue flame dancing on the dragon decoration of the Aizen's helmet makes the dragon seem to writhe and stamp as if living; the feathers of the demon's *kabuto* helmet waver with his every motion. After a polite exchange the Aizen tells the demon chief that the Kishimo has come and will join them in making their way through the Sea of Mists to the land of Tsunu.

To the Kishimo is explained, by the Aizen and the demon chief, the name and nature of these beings.

They are the *shikome;* he is called Ibaraki.

They have fled from the island of Onogoro, driven away by cataclysm and lost, forever seeking to find their abandoned home and reclaim it. Their chieftain Ibaraki seeks more than the return to Onogoro. First he must recover his hand. Kishimo gazes at the armored sleeves of Ibaraki and sees in truth that one of them ends in a living organ, the other in a clever work of armor, a *tekko,* hand guard, made to work like a living hand.

The samurai Yorimutso took my hand, Ibaraki tells the Kishimo. I placed it upon his shoulder as he dozed beside the Rashomon gate; I thought to play a prank on the sleeper but he played a prank upon me instead. With his long *katana* sword he took my hand. My fine hand with its precious claws. *Ah!* Behold my fine claws!

He holds forth his true hand for Kishimo and the Aizen to see. The claws are indeed long, gracefully curved like those of a cat, as sharp as five daggers, as polished as lacquer. Kishimo shudders and feels a tingling in the flesh of her back.

Ibaraki holds forth his *tekko;* its careful iron workmanship and green-tied braid create the appearance of a hand, but within there is only blackness and hollowness.

Ah! I will have back my hand! Ibaraki exclaims. I will have back my hand from the samurai Yorimutso! Such a clever fellow! Such a fine joker!

He laughs and claps himself upon the shoulders, the hollow *tekko* clattering when it strikes his spear shaft of lacquered wood.

A fine joke, eh?

Onogoro? the Kishimo asks.

The first land! When the god and the goddess, Izanami and Izanagi, plunged the tip of their finest spear into the sea, in the early time when there was no land in the world, the island Onogoro congealed about the tip of their spear. My people, the *shikome,* populated Onogoro. It must be ours once more—if only we could find it. Another splendid joke, eh? He doubles with laughter.

The Kishimo turns to Aizen and asks the reason for their presence here in the cavern of the *shikome.*

The *shikome,* he explains, are his allies. They possess a power which they share with him, the Aizen, and which he will share with the woman Kishimo.

Together they will sail *Ofuna* safely over the Sea of Mists: Aizen and Kishimo, Miroku, the sailors above and *shikome* below.

Ah! Ah! the demon chieftain wails. The Sea of Mists is fraught with perils. Its great storms are to be feared. There are pirates who sail its surface, ready to greet those few travelers who survive the winds and waves with swords and shafts. And beneath the waters of the sea there are others, beings half fish, half man, who greet sailors for reasons of their own.

But now? What to do now?

The Aizen courteously requests Ibaraki to cast a powder into the blue flame. The *shikome* chieftain nods, rises, bows, makes his way back to his people. They shuffle and bow to their king, they mumble and chant when he speaks to them.

From among them a pair emerge, bows slung over their shoulders, carrying a heavy lacquered chest between them. No sign does Kishimo see of the source of the chest. It is carved and decorated with the flowers and beasts of myth, its metalwork formed into dragons and foxes, badgers and boars.

The two *shikome* bow to Ibaraki. He bends and opens the chest, scoops dust from within it with his iron *tekko* hand. The *shikome* retainers clamp shut the lacquered chest and disappear with it. Kishimo does not see where it goes.

Ibaraki bounds to the edge of the rock fissure. He bows

deeply toward the flame. Behind him, all his people do likewise. Aizen and Kishimo also bow.

All rise.

With his iron *tekko* hand, Ibaraki makes a pass through the dancing ultramarine column.

The flame flares up and outward from the fissure, climbing to three times its normal height, spreading like a great bowl to envelop the clustered *shikome*. And now it lapses back to its former state, twisting and leaping above the opening in the rock, and in it Kishimo sees the Aizen, elevated and illuminated, hovering and turning in the glowing azure air above the fissure.

His eyes stare blankly, his hands hang loosely at his sides, the *daisho*, paired longsword and dirk, remain undrawn in their twin lacquered scabbards.

About the Aizen, Kishimo sees other figures, ghostly, whirling, rising like sprites from the fissure of the flame, writhing and turning about the body of the Aizen. The blue flame dances over his armor and above his body, reflecting in the dragon ornament of his *hoshi-kabuto*, star-decorated helmet.

The mouth of the Aizen opens and from it pour sounds that are to the ears of the Kishimo faint and remote, as if they were beating to her from a great distance or even were crossing the boundaries of ancient time. The Aizen wears no *hoate* or *mempo*, no metal armored mask of the type used to protect a samurai's face from the blows of a foeman's arrows or sword. The Kishimo sees the face of Aizen widen in wonder—and in horror—at whatever it is that the man-god has been shown within the flame.

The *shikome* exclaim in awe and cover their faces at the sight of Aizen dancing in the flame overhead; their king Ibaraki grins at the vision.

At length the flaring flame drops low and the Aizen descends as if lowered by a giant hand to the rock beside the fissure. The Aizen stands unmoving for long moments while the *shikome*, squatting and mumbling around the fissure, watch without response.

Now the Aizen strides toward Kishimo and Ibaraki.

Ibaraki the king of the *shikome* bows low before the Aizen. The Aizen gestures to Ibaraki and Kishimo; they settle themselves in lotus position, the woman with graceful limbs and supple torso, the *shikome* a bandy-legged and squat-bodied parody beside her. Behind and about them the *shikome* shuffle and grumble, drawing their circle more closely about the three but retaining a space of bare rock floor between them.

The Aizen nods to Kishimo and to Ibaraki.

Did you receive a vision? the *shikome* inquires.

The Aizen moves one hand and nods his head, the dragon on his helmet catching in its jeweled eyes the flare of the ultramarine fire; the dragon shimmers blue, its forked tongue flickering out and back between its rows of needle teeth.

The Aizen speaks:

I received the vision of the blue flame. As I received the vision one other time, peering into another realm, and saw there the Kishimo. Now I peered through the mists of time and the reaches of distance, not into any other realm than this, yet seeing things which are not here and events which are not yet.

I rose above the Sea of Mists. I saw *Ofuna* beating her way through sleet and gale, her sailors chill and beaten on her decks yet striving to perform their tasks. I saw an opening in the storm, *Ofuna* reaching waters where no sleet fell, where winds and waves were lower than those of the Sea of Mists.

And here I saw—others. My vision was not clear. I saw other ships, but not whose they were. I saw *Ofuna* caught between two foes, arrows arching and havoc spread across her decks. I saw boarders met with lance and sword and dagger, blood pouring upon the decks of *Ofuna* and spilling into the waters of the Sea of Mists.

I heard the cries of the dying and the crash of metal. I saw the battle ended but I did not see its outcome: who was the victor, who the vanquished.

Then I saw no more.

Ah! grunts Ibaraki. You see but you cannot tell the meaning of your vision! You are betrayed by the powder and betrayed by the flame. *Ah!*

The Aizen turns toward Kishimo. He asks if she would try to read the vision of the flame.

She cannot read his vision, she says. She cannot read the vision that was given to another, for she cannot see what he saw, she can merely hear his words as he tells of what he saw.

For the first time the king of the *shikome*, Ibaraki, addresses words to Kishimo. Can the woman not see the vision? Does she fear the flame? Or does she fear to be illumined?

Kishimo rises, her face hot, conscious of her woman's body beneath the thin kimono, dried now by the heat of the blue dancing flame. With thumb and forefinger of one hand she presses against her chest, drawing the flesh tight. I will try to see the vision, she cries. She rises to her feet and stands beside Ibaraki. Even as the demon stands, his head reaches little above the waist of the woman. I will try to see the vision, she tells him again.

Ibaraki signals to his retainers and they return with the glistening lacquered casket. Ibaraki lifts from it a handful of powder, using his iron hand to perform the task: using his *tekko*.

He returns to the side of the Kishimo and gazes up into her face. She returns his stare. His eyes are great and dark and in their depths the twisting blue fires catch sparks that dance back at Kishimo.

The demon king Ibaraki takes Kishimo by the hand—she sees that he uses his living hand, not his *tekko,* for this, and she feels a surge of relief. He leads her to stand beside the fissure in the rock. He releases her hand and circles the fissure, halting opposite her position and sweeping his *tekko,* his iron hand, through the flame between them, sifting the powder between the metal fingers of the *tekko* and into the flame.

Again the ultramarine flares upward and outward, covering the assembled *shikome* like a great tent, then falling back upon itself, yet lifting her, lifting the Kishimo, from the rock floor and floating her like a hovering gull upon a rising column of warm ocean air.

She gazes about herself and sees the distant glowing specks of other fires rising from the rock, the distant wood, the distant water. She looks beneath and sees only brilliance, ultramarine brilliance, streaming up at her, lifting her, streaming at her. She sees wraith-like forms dancing and whirling upward toward her through the flame. The fire flares again and she is blinded for a moment; then her vision clears and she can see a great city stretched beneath her feet, tall buildings and wide avenues, people by the thousands moving about, a gorgeous snow-capped mountain in the distance beyond the city.

She hears the crackling of the blue flame and yet through it she hears the tiny hum and clamor of the city beneath her. The sun shines brightly, the sky sparkles with a color of blue as disparate from the tincture of the flame as is the white of freshly fallen snow from that of rich cream.

The city bustles, its people scurry, and through the air above it a speck is moving, buzzing and gleaming in the glorious sunlight, buzzing and glinting as it draws nearer to the center of the city, passes over it, and suddenly the city erupts into a glory of red and white and gold, a globe of splendor rising from its center, growing and glowing with inner fires.

The ball of flame heaves and rolls and climbs, and far behind it there follows a sound, a crack and roar and boom and a howling that passes about the Kishimo, leaving her untouched and unfeeling, dazzled by the glory and wonder of the sight she has beheld. The golden flame surrounds her and transfigures her into a living creation of crimson and gold and then slowly it fades away, leaving her bathed once more in the glaring ultramarine.

She feels herself floating, floating slowly and gently downward until her slippered feet touch the rock beside the fissure of the flame and she stumbles once, then recovers and strides away from the fissure and approaches the Aizen and the *shikome* king Ibaraki; the heart within her breast glows and pounds and the Aizen and the *shikome* chieftain bow before her. She is bathed in an aura of blue with flickering flamelets of gold and crimson; her halo lights the Aizen and Ibaraki with dancing lights.

The Aizen asks if she was in truth illumined.

Kishimo nods her head.

He asks if she will reveal her vision.

She nods again and speaks.

She tells all that she has seen. The Aizen asks if she knows the city, the meaning of the globe of golden flame.

Kishimo shakes her head.

Nor I, states the Aizen; Nor I, states the *shikome* king.

The clustered *shikome* shuffle and sway; they send up a wailing; their king Ibaraki turns and faces them; he raises and shakes his *naginata* spear, holding it in his iron *tekko* hand.

Howling, the demons draw and brandish weapons: spears, lances, bows and arrows, stamping their feet and roaring at the top of their voices.

The rock floor trembles. The blue flame wavers. Ibaraki the demon chief shouts. Aizen the man-god gestures, the dragon upon his iron helmet glinting and shimmering.

The Aizen holds his doeskin-gloved hands in the shimmering blue column and the cavernous place darkens and shakes. The dim distances grow misty, the rock floor is transformed into planking, the fissure is closed and the flame is gone.

Kishimo is surrounded by the clash of metal, the shouts of men. She stands on the deck of *Ofuna*. She stands in the midst of battle.

6

Kishimo turns toward the Aizen to ask how they came here but he himself is gone. She stands upon the quarterdeck again: alone. On the decks below her, sailors, *shikome,* and water *kappa* are joined in battle. Cries of challenge, clash of weapons and of armor, shrieks of the wounded, moans of the dying.

The sleet has ceased to fall—or *Ofuna,* at any rate, has found a breach in the storm. The sky is still gray with heavy, rolling clouds, but the light is stronger. The air is less wet but it is colder than ever. The sea is black and throws hungry fingers of white foam at the hull of *Ofuna.*

In the darkling day, black-painted ships have joined battle with *Ofuna,* casting flights of arrows against her crewmen, speeding through the sheltering mist until they approach her from either side. *Ofuna'*s sailors have raced below, donned armor, seized weapons, pounded back to face their attackers.

One ship of foes has rammed *Ofuna,* its bowsprit a carved monster covered with cast iron, crashing through *Ofuna'*s hull, grapnels and ropes following, *kappa* racing from the deck of the attacker to that of *Ofuna.*

Kappa—the sea-sprites of infamous repute. As fierce as *shikome* yet cleverer, wittier, mischievous; formed like men, they fight with unmatched strength and courage, yet they have an oddity that offers the hope of escape or even of victory to their foes. Their heads are oddly formed, their skulls concave. The water-beings carry tiny ponds with them, balanced carefully on their heads. These are their link with the sea, the source of their strength. Spill the water and the *kappa* lapses into weakness, helplessness. They may be bound, beaten, destroyed —or set free on ransom of pledge for some future deeds.

The *kappa* have swarmed the decks of *Ofuna* and now they engage her defenders with sword, dirk, lance. Kishimo sees none of her few acquaintances: Miroku, Aizen, Ibaraki. The infant king and captain of *Ofuna* may still be below, awaiting in his cabin the outcome of the engagement. The man-god and the *shikome* lord must be engaged in the struggle with the *kappa*, but they are not to be seen from the quarterdeck where Kishimo stands.

There is a terrible cry—*Aiiee!*—and Kishimo starts, whirls, sees a monstrous *kappa* dressed in filthy rags and sandals. He cocks his arm, drawing back his lance. The moment is frozen for Kishimo: she sees the *kappa*, the battle raging about him, the bloodied decks of *Ofuna*, the fastened *kappa* ship and gray-black sea with its layers of whirling mist.

The *kappa*'s weapon has a long shaft banded with rings of copper and lacquered wood, silken tassels and cruciform blade of the *magari-yari* type, its plum-leaf-shaped main blade and pointed arms mounted to pierce and destroy the enemy. The pounding heart within the breast of Kishimo throbs heavily as the moment of frozen time is past.

The arm of the *kappa* sweeps forward. The *magari-yari* lance flies away from the *kappa*, forward and upward. Its streaming silken tassels snap in the frigid air. The shaft whizzes over the railing that surrounds the quarterdeck. Kishimo sweeps a doeskin-gloved hand upward and catches the lance directly behind the head. Her fingers capture the metal rings of the shaft. The cruciform blade glitters and hisses a finger's width from the center of Kishimo's breast. She laughs and reverses the lance, holding it at the ready, its *magari-yari* blade primed now to do her own bidding.

A look of startlement crosses the face of the *kappa*; a gasp of surprise escapes his ugly lips.

The *kappa* reaches to the sash of his tattered kimono and

draws from it a battered *katana* sword. The sash is an ancient *obi,* torn and bloodied in past battles. The *katana* is rusted and dull to the eye, as much a club as a sword by now.

The lip of Kishimo curls in disdain for the *kappa.*

Still, the *kappa* races to the flight leading from the main deck of *Ofuna* to the quarterdeck where Kishimo waits. He all but flies from the lower planking to the risers. At the head of the stairs he halts, facing Kishimo. The *kappa* bows, a strange, grotesque movement in which he holds his head upright to keep the pond of water on his skull.

Kishimo, holding the lance in both her *yugake,* doeskin gloves, returns the water-sprite's courtesy.

Before she arises he is upon her, swinging the marred *katana* sword in both his gnarled hands. The blow is aimed at Kishimo's arm. She parries the blow with the shaft of her lance; the blade of the *katana* rebounds from the metal rings of the lance, a dull resonation rising with the clash of metal upon metal. From the sound, Kishimo knows that the *katana* is of fine steel; if cleaned, reforged, rehoned, its lost fineness might be restored still.

Kishimo swings the shaft of her lance, using it as a quarterstaff, striking the *kappa* alongside his ear. He bounds sideways, nimbly twisting to retain the water atop his concave skull. He feints with his *katana,* jabbing as if to pierce the kimono of Kishimo at the waist and split her bowels with his blade. She moves the lance to block the blow but instead the *kappa* swings his blade against Kishimo's head.

She apprehends the maneuver and drops her head, bending her knees to avoid the blow. She succeeds in part; the dull blade crashes into her *han-buri,* her headband of heavy cloth. The headband and Kishimo's own thick dark hair protect her skull from the blow of the *katana.* The dullness of the *kappa*'s blade aids the woman as well.

For an instant her sight blackens and flowers of white and rose dance before her eyes, but very quickly she recovers. The water-sprite too is recovering from his move; the woman staggers and regains her balance. Her gloved hands grasp the shaft of her lance more tightly than ever.

She launches a terrible blow at the *kappa*. The sprite's arms are extended, his hands clutching the long hilt of his battered sword. Kishimo plunges the *magari-yari* lance downward. (The *kappa,* like the demon *shikome,* are squat creatures; Kishimo is tall and straight.) The cruciform blade of the lance plunges between the opened elbows of the *kappa*. The plum-leaf-shaped blade pierces his filthy kimono and buries itself in his belly. The pointed arms of the blade pierce his skin also, preventing the blade from penetrating through the *kappa*'s body and emerging from his back.

The sprite yields up a horrible scream of pain and fear. His mouth falls open, his eyes stare wildly. A spasm of his muscles and he pulls away from Kishimo. She holds tightly to her lance. The *kappa* spills backward from Kishimo and tumbles down the flight leading from the quarterdeck to the battle below.

The *kappa,* writhing and screaming, disappears beneath the struggling feet of sailors and demons as they battle on the deck of the ship *Ofuna.*

Kishimo, flushed with her triumph, plunges down the flight after the *kappa*. She knows that the crew of *Ofuna* are her allies, the attackers her foes. The sailors are now wearing *keiko* armor, iron plates rather than lamellar; many have iron helmets also, of varied design; a few wear the metal *hoate* or *mempo* masks to protect them from blows.

The *shikome* disdain armor. They wear as few clothes as do the *kappa,* and attack fiercely with sword, dirk, or lance. They do not retreat.

Kishimo confronts a fighter wielding lizard-skin *tanto,* a short sword, its steel blade decorated with *horimono,* engravings of armed *sennin,* wise man with sword and flame. The foeman slashes at Kishimo; she parries with her *magari-yari,* cracks her enemy on thin leather cuirass with hilt of her lance. He recovers and delivers a blow to her body. She dodges and receives a long scratch through her kimono along the ribs of her side. But now her opponent is far extended, his blade in major part beyond the body of Kishimo.

She draws back her *magari-yari,* drives its plum-leaf-shaped blade between the *hoate* metal mask and the leather cuirass of her enemy. The blade pierces his windpipe and jugular. With a single gasp and a gout of blood he falls.

Kishimo sees the tide of battle flow and ebb. She sees boarders now carrying the struggle back to the attacker's ship. She holds her cruciform-bladed lance close at her side, trots in slippers across the blood-running deck of *Ofuna;* hot gore mixes with freezing sleet to make the planking treacherous beneath her feet.

She reaches the edge of the deck, seizes an iron, barb-tipped grapnel from the raider, and climbs atop the rail. The bowsprit of the raiding ship is beneath her feet; in the rough water it rocks and *Ofuna* pitches. The ironwork of the bowsprit is ripping still at *Ofuna*'s hull, enlarging the hole it produced when it rammed Miroku's craft.

Kishimo places her feet on the edge of *Ofuna*'s rail, using a roughly woven grappling line for traction. Below her is the deck of the raider. Holding her lance in both hands as a balancing pole, she leaps from *Ofuna* to the deck of the raider.

As she sails through the thin gray air there is a crack above and lightning pierces the dark clouds that scud over the Sea of Mists. The sleet, which had ceased for a brief time to fall, resumes. The air grows colder. The falling flakes are no longer the soft half-melted blobs of watery slush but hard opaque pellets of ice: hail.

Kishimo, on the deck of the raider, turns back to see the condition aboard *Ofuna.* The day has darkened and murky figures struggle and shift about the deck. Cries are still heard; the tide of battle cannot be read.

On board the deck of the raider ship, Kishimo sees that the fighting has moved away from the rail. There are no fighters near her. The air is cold, cold, and the rattling hailstones are covering the decks with a thick layer of white. Kishimo peers into the dimness. The sound of battle has receded: there are no sailors, no *kappa,* no *shikome* to be seen near her. She looks above to see the sails of the raider craft silhouetted black against the nearly black sky that pelts down stones of ice.

Kishimo hefts her cruciform-bladed lance and strides toward the stern of the raider ship. The sounds of battle are softer now. Those coming from behind her on *Ofuna* echo remote and faint, distant and high above, muffled by the hiss of falling hail and the rattle of striking stones. The sounds of battle aboard the raider ship are softened, too, by the sounds of nature and the ghostly darkness descending upon the ship.

Kishimo strides toward the stern.

She comes upon a sailor lying face down on the deck, the hail beginning already to cover him with a white coating. Kishimo kneels beside him. The sailor does not move. With an effort the woman heaves him over onto his back. There is a dark area on the deck where he has lain. Now he lies stretched on icy whiteness.

His eyes are open with horror, his face contorted with pain. His breast is ripped wide. His hand still clenches a *tachi,* long sword, its hilt wound with scarlet silk, its blade marked with *horimono* of dragon and thunderbolt. The blade is bloody.

Laying her lance aside for a moment, Kishimo uncurls the dead sailor's fingers from about the hilt of the fine-worked *tachi.* He wears a scarlet-painted scabbard held by an *uwa-obi,* outer belt. She loosens his belt and ties it with the scarlet-painted scabbard about her waist, over her kimono.

As she takes the *obi* from the dead sailor there is a clatter, and a *yoroi-doshi,* an armor-piercing blade, falls from the *obi* to the ice-covered deck. Kishimo retrieves the *yoroi-doshi* and tucks it into the *obi* once more, this time for her own use should a need occur.

With doeskin-gloved fingers she closes the eyes of the sailor. Then she rises to make her way from him and strides farther aft. The ship is in nearly total silence now. The voices have ceased, the clash and shouts of battle are no longer heard. Kishimo passes many bodies—sailors, *shikome, kappa,* the three mixed carelessly, their blood mingling and freezing with the frozen hail upon the black-lacquered deck of the raider.

The cold is more intense than ever. The hail hisses and

clatters, hisses and clatters. The ship's coating of gleaming white ice has grown as deep as a woman's foot. Kishimo's slippers grip the ice well where the fresh hail gives it a rough and pebbled surface; less well where any shelter or warmth has given rise to a smoother face.

She hears no voices, no clash of steel on armor.

The darkness reveals only the glowing ghostly tints of ice. The black deck is white, smooth, and clear, save where long mounds mark fallen warriors. The ship's railings, lines, shrouds, masts, sheets—white, white.

The sky is black, and from it falls white.

There is a rending sound, a crack and boom. Kishimo runs back toward the prow of the raider ship. The metal-worked bowsprit has broken away from *Ofuna;* the grapnels, lacking the support of the rammed bowsprit, have fallen away. Through the dark air Kishimo gazes back toward *Ofuna*. She sees what may be the ship, its outline obscured by sheets of falling hail. She calls to *Ofuna* and her voice echoes feebly, muffled by the falling hail as it hisses on the face of the sea and clatters on the decks of the black ship.

The gray form of *Ofuna* glides silently away into the darkness. Kishimo stands on the prow of the raider ship, feeling the chill of air and hail on her shoulders and arms. The breath in her chest is like an icy fist clutching at her heart.

The shawl of the Aizen is draped about her shoulders still, covering her kimono. She clutches it more closely about her and turns back to survey the raider ship. It is ghostly white now, its coat of ice covering all lacquer, all wood, all canvas. The masts of the ship point like skeletal hands toward the black sky. The railings are thick and white like glistening bloated mold.

The sea all about the ship is black.

The only sound is the steady hiss of hail upon water, the constant rattle of hail upon ice.

Kishimo brushes white crust from her hair and face and draws the shawl over her head for protection. The hail rebounds from the cloth, popping and snapping with each strike.

Scabbarded *tachi* and *yoroi-doshi* thrust through her *obi*, cross-bladed *jumonji-yari* in hand, she makes her way to a hatch. She uses the blade of her lance to chop away crusted ice until a door is exposed and she manages to heave it open with the full weight and strength of her body. To gain what small light remains on the deck of the ship, she leaves the bulkhead open and makes her way below.

Within the raider, all is covered with ice. How could this be? wonders Kishimo. The sleet and hail could hardly have penetrated the interior of the ship. A great hole below the water line might have permitted this much water to enter and then to freeze. Kishimo edges through a narrow companionway. The fittings of the ship are sparse and covered with white. The air is dank, moist; its odor is heavy with the scent of marine weeds.

Kishimo finds her way to the hold. The ship is not as dark within as she had expected. There is a glow, so faint and so pale as to defy understanding. It comes from within the ice or seems to, not lighting the hold itself but rather giving each object a ghastly illumination of its own.

Weapons, stacks of armor, furs, plate of precious metals. All coated with ice. All glowing faintly. The hold of the raider is deathly silent. The air is bitter and chilled. The roll and sway of the ship is constant.

Kishimo turns to leave the hold. By her feet she observes a thin, steady trickle of dark water. Its source is unseen—it may be trickling from the deck of the raider, or seeping through ill-caulked boards or from some unknown gash in the hull beneath the water line. Kishimo cannot find the source.

The companionway that had brought her to the raider's hold is more heavily iced than ever. Kishimo tries to push her way from the hold of the ship. The walls of the companionway have closed. The space between them is less broad than her shoulders. The deck has risen, the headway lowered. She can only squeeze into the still narrowing passage and squirm through like a snake in its burrow, wriggling and pushing.

She draws her breath deeply and presses herself into the narrow opening. A cold trickle of water penetrates the cloth of her kimono and breeches and outrages her flesh with icy intimacy. She stretches her arms ahead of herself like a swimmer and slides her torso ahead. She draws deep mouthfuls of dank air and exhales forcefully, thrusting ahead with hands, pressing with elbows and feet, sliding her body through the opening.

Where the companionway arches upward toward the deck of the raider she presses harder than ever, gaining some extra purchase against the ice behind her, fighting against the slipperiness higher up.

She reaches the end of the ice tunnel.

It is frozen shut.

She rubs the inner surface of the ice with her doeskin *yugake,* clearing the ice sufficiently to see through it. Beyond, as though through a frosted panel, she can observe the deck of the raider, the crusted railing, the swollen deck, the mounds of white that mark the bodies of dead warriors.

She thrusts at the blockage with her lance. Its plum-leaf-shaped blade pierces the ice, cracking it into a cobweb of green-tinted white. She draws back on the lance and strikes again, again, yet again, with each plunge of the blade gouging new bits of ice from the heavy sheet that has imprisoned her. She finds that the work of chopping at the ice has warmed her body, drawing perspiration from her face and shoulders while still her legs and feet are trapped in the icy passage behind her, numbed of all sensation.

The air in her prison is becoming stale, dank, unsatisfying.

She thrusts with the lance and another chip of ice flies from the face of the blockage. Her efforts have marred the smooth surface of the ice, so she cannot see beyond nor determine the thickness of the pane. She strikes once more with her blade, and once more a shard of ice flies from the pane, and bounds from the shawl covering her shoulder.

She gasps for air, clenches her teeth, and squeezes her eyes shut, gathering her strength. She draws back her shoulders and heaves forward again, plunging the plum-leaf-shaped blade into the ice. The blade pierces farther than she had expected. Kishimo draws it back and sees through the small opening the exterior of the raider.

Long work refreshed with new air drawn through the opening, and Kishimo emerges, bedraggled, onto the deck of the raider ship. Behind her she observes the tunnel from which she has emerged. The opening is narrow and even though its mouth has been cleared she cannot see more than the length of her *tachi,* longsword, into the depths of the ship.

Even as she watches, the slow trickle of water inching down the tunnel, freezing as it moves, thickens the bottom of the opening. Astonishingly soon the tunnel of ice is completely closed, filled with whiteness. There is no longer a passage into the hold of the raider. The ship is full of ice.

Kishimo paces once about the deck of the ship. The sky above is still utterly black, the hail is falling more softly now and trending back toward the sleet that had hissed down earlier.

The waters about the hull are fairly quiet, and the wind has ceased utterly.

There is nothing to be seen but black water, black sky, distant banks of mist shifting and hissing their way across the surface of the sea.

Using the plum-shaped blade of her lance in one hand and the *yoroi-doshi* armor piercer taken from the body of the dead raider warrior in the other, she climbs the slippery, ice-coated flight to the quarterdeck of the raider craft. Here is more whiteness, more silence.

She finds a long mound of white, and, using her *yugake* -gloved hands to clear and smooth its surface, she sees lying within the frozen, helmeted form of the Aizen.

7

Kishimo draws her *yoroi-doshi* and leans across the ice-encased Aizen. She raises her blade to strike at the ice and works to free the man-god. How he came here she does not know. What lies before her she knows no more, but only that the Aizen has aided her before now. Thus—despite the warning of the Miroku that the Aizen is a foe, Kishimo wonders: Is he the foe of the Miroku only, or mine as well?

She grasps the braid-tied hilt of the *yoroi-doshi* in two gloved hands and swings it toward the Aizen. The armor-piercing knife descends toward the ice-encased Aizen and swings aside, its point lodging in the ice covering the quarterdeck beside the Aizen. The Kishimo is startled. She wrests the blade away from the ice and raises it once more to strike.

But instead she stays her hands and gazes into the face of the Aizen. It lies beneath clear ice, the dragon-decorated, *hoshi*-starred helmet in place, the armor of the Aizen undamaged.

The eyes, dark and wide, stare up at Kishimo through the ice. There is a compelling force within those eyes. They speak to Kishimo; they command her actions.

Slowly she lowers the *yoroi-doshi,* restores it to its place in its scabbard in her *obi.* Instead of chopping the ice that imprisons the Aizen, Kishimo removes the shawl from her shoulders and drops it beside the mound of ice covering his body.

Hardly conscious of her own actions, she places longsword

and shorter armor piercer, plum-leaf-bladed lance also, beside
the long narrow mound. With stiff fingers she unties her *obi,*
peels kimono from her body. Sleet plasters itself to her naked
flesh; Kishimo shudders, the jolt of motion running from
shoulders to feet.

Gazing into the ice-shrouded eyes of the Aizen, she climbs
upon his frozen bier and lowers herself, arms held wide, legs
open, onto the ice. Its gleaming surface clings to her nakedness;
the shock of its frigid touch pierces her like a million frozen
needles. An involuntary gasp escapes her. Cold air floods her
recovering lungs, driving down against tense diaphragm.

She buries the side of her face in the ice covering that of the
Aizen; she feels as if she were sinking into the ice, the life-flame
of her body is drawn through the ice to the form of the Aizen.
Water runs over her body and dribbles away, over the edges of
the Aizen's bier, to run briefly onto the ship's black deck before
freezing once again.

Rapidly the ice separating Kishimo's naked flesh from the
armored body beneath her melts away. With another shock she
finds the rough cords and hard plates of the Aizen's armor
cutting into her nudity. She springs from the bier and clutches
her kimono and breeches and weapons from the icy deck
before they too are frozen solid, then she advances to stand
once more over the body of the man-god. The eyes flicker and
command. Kishimo reaches with one *yugake*-gloved hand and
touches the hand armor of the Aizen.

The Aizen's hand, gloved and metal-cased, rises slowly as the
Kishimo stands paralyzed. Fingers reach to press her soft breast.
From the point of contact she feels a terrible pulsation drive
through her, flame and frost in one, sending her blood pulsing
dizzyingly through her belly and limbs.

The Aizen withdraws his hand.

Kishimo stands, feeling momentarily drained of life, but slowly
she recovers herself.

Aizen rises: sits upright, bends and raises one knee, pushes
himself first to kneel, then to stand before Kishimo. You have
my thanks, he tells her . . . you have the gratitude of the Aizen.

Kishimo bows her head in response.

The Aizen places an armored hand beneath her chin and raises her face with slight pressure. The armor covering his hand is harsh. Kishimo watches Aizen as he surveys the raider ship. He throws back his shoulders, strides about the quarterdeck looking in all directions. At length he returns to stand before Kishimo.

You have been below, he says inquiringly.

Kishimo says that she has. She details her escape from the clogging ice belowdecks.

Aizen asks if she has seen any living being on board this ship. She has not.

He nods, raises hand to jaw. He is illumined by the faint, diffuse light of the ice surrounding them. He strides from Kishimo, raises both his hands, holding them above the level of his shoulders as if in communion with some unseen force, but he does not speak. For a long time he stands this way.

Through the dimness above the Sea of Mists, Kishimo hears a great flying creature approach. In the darkness she can see nothing beyond the tall masts and spars of the ship, shimmering within their ghostly envelopes of ice. But sound penetrates the darkness: the whir and flap of great wings, the soft burring sounds of the creature itself.

Suddenly appearing with a gust of cold air that batters Kishimo against the deck of the raider, the creature drops onto the ice, nuzzling with its giant head against the side of the Aizen, careless of his weapons, his armor. The man-god strokes and embraces the head of the great beast. He speaks to it endearingly: *Oh, ah, oh!*

The Aizen faces the Kishimo. To remain here, he says, would be to spend eternity in an icy limbo. This he does not wish for his own fate, but that of Kishimo is for her to decide. Will she remain? Will she fly with him?

Kishimo does not speak for a moment. It is the first time that the Aizen has offered her any choice. Until now he has simply commanded, and she, not knowing why, has obeyed. Now he offers a choice—but what choice: to remain aboard the black ship; to be frozen in the grip of time; to drift forever, icebound, silent in the Sea of Mists.

She knows not the origin of this raider craft, nor the fate of all its crew. Was every *kappa* killed in the battle against *Ofuna?* Did none survive? Have any returned to their watery realm? What fate has overtaken *Ofuna,* Miroku, Ibaraki?

How did the Aizen become frozen as he was when Kishimo found him?

Questions! There are questions and questions but there are no answers—surely none to be found aboard a frozen raider craft adrift in the Sea of Mists.

I will accompany the Aizen, Kishimo says at last.

The great beast appears to understand the words of Kishimo. It lays its great head against her while she caresses its bulging skull, as if she were a peasant mistress and it a happy cat. It seems almost to purr.

The Aizen and the Kishimo climb onto the back of the huge beast and it leaps from the frozen quarterdeck as it has done before. Once again the creature beats its mighty wings and rises into blackness. Beneath them Kishimo observes the luminous, ice-coated raider. It becomes ever smaller as they climb into the still sky.

Once more the creature folds its wings to its sides. Again it tilts and falls through the air; Kishimo's hair streams from under her *han-buri* and snaps behind her; the rushing air screams in her ears. As they speed toward the chill waters, the glowing raider flashes by, sparkling figures appearing to dance upon black decks, and then there is the icy spume once more, the sense of darkness and water all about, the moment of panic fear as Kishimo's breath, exhausted, rushes outward in fragile bubbles, the moment of choking and gagging as the icy water penetrates Kishimo's throat and her lungs, and finally the astonishing euphoria as she realizes that she can breathe this water.

Is it so densely saturated with oxygen that her lungs gain nourishment from it? Is her body, like that of some old dipnoan fish, able to strain water as well as air? Or is this some effect created by the Aizen through a power unknown to Kishimo, unexplained and unmentioned but exercised by the man-god to permit this woman her survival?

As it has before, the beast carries the Aizen and the Kishimo through regions of dimness and disorientation, waters in which there is neither interface of sea to air above nor of sea to solid sea bottom beneath. The very notion of *up* and that of *down* lose their meanings; to the Kishimo there is only the beast beneath herself and herself upon the beast.

Marine creatures flicker by: luminous fish of every color and description, long and slim, armored as if for war, massive and powerful, fiercely toothed, marked in glowing yellows and reds and luminous blues, some transparently fleshed like living skeletons swaying and fleeting past, some jelly-like, some with strange luminous organs gleaming like lanterns through the gloom; some, marine reptiles, armored tortoises, and scaled water snakes, their eyes peering coldly at the amazing vision of the winged beast with its male and its female rider; skates and rays with rippling wings: gray, yellow-white, mottled green and brown; arachnids browsing placidly, safe within their shells jointed like the lamellar armor of a samurai.

Like a cold-blooded marine creature herself, the Kishimo has felt neither chill nor warmth in the water but now a frigid zone is reached that penetrates to the very marrow of her bones. Her skin shrivels with the cold.

Still there is no up or down; the water is lighted faintly but Kishimo detects no source of the light: a sun penetrating from above—wherever that might be—its rays diffused beyond detection of their origin; the cumulative illumination of uncounted marine creatures; the water itself, suffused with some ingredient that emits a faint but regular glow. . . .

Specks of white appear in the distance. The beast approaches them: irregular chunks of ice tumbling and drifting in the seemingly universal fluid. To Kishimo it seems that this may be the end of all things: neither in fire nor in dust but in an immanent flood that reduces space and objects to ultimate homogeneity.

But that sameness is broken by the tumbling ice bodies.

The beast draws near to them and sweeps past shards, between and among them, while Kishimo peers into the whiteness of them and sees that the opacity of many is broken by a clarity that permits her to glimpse within, to perceive vistas inside, universes contained:

A warrior, armored and bearing longbow, *yanagi-ba,* willow-leaf-shaped arrowheads, *urakigo no kabuto,* chrysanthemum-back helmet. He has drawn and nocked an arrow and glares fiercely at an unseen foe.

A great lens-shaped nebula, its center exploding, glowing with overwhelming brilliance, the blade-like edges as yet untouched but irretrievably doomed.

A mountainside thronged with thousands of pilgrims come to hear some *sutra,* the guru feeding his great multitude of chelas from a tiny store of loaves and fish.

A monster as great as a ship gazing placidly about itself, suddenly shadowed by huge jagged wings, swept away to be devoured by a creature to whom it is itself a mere dwarf.

A structure as high as clouds, its peak shining like a beacon through the night, struck with a bolt from above and reduced to glowing ashes in the instant.

A battle of armadas fitted with terrible weapons that belch fire and hurl great metal boulders to smash and rend one another from distances beyond the horizon.

A mighty beast that swims through a watery world, propelling itself with long, veined wings and many legs; on its back, a god-like male and a female in kimono and breeches, her hair long and jet-black, sweeping behind her from beneath a knotted *han-buri.* With an electrifying jolt the Kishimo locks eyes with the woman of the other world, the woman seen in the ice block.

How do I appear to her? the Kishimo wonders. Am I, is the Aizen, is our beast . . . seen frozen in a timeless instant within the confines of a tumbling block of ice, while that other Kishimo, that other Aizen, that other beast swim through some alien realm beneath another Sea of Mists? Is that other Kishimo my sister? My image? Is she myself?

The beast sweeps the water with its great veined wings. Its legs hurl it forward through the gloom.

The ice tumbles and falls behind them now, for while there is neither *down* nor *up,* yet there remain *before* and *behind.*

The Aizen prods the great beast with his own *yoroi-doshi.* The beast is unharmed by the prodding but understands it as a sign from its master. It rears once, lifting its head so that a looming faceted eye glares back at the Aizen; then the creature swings its wings, one upward, one downward, and enters a new course, a long helical curve that threatens with each sweep to dislodge Kishimo and hurl her from her place on its back.

Kishimo clutches the beast with knees and ankles, holding to the Aizen with her arms as swoop follows dizzyingly upon swoop. Somewhere beyond the circumference of the expanding helix, the dim luminosity of the water increases and Kishimo fixes her gaze upon the area of light.

Great fronds of greenery reach like long flexible fingers from the region of light toward the beast with its two riders. Now the beast reorients itself so that its legs dangle toward the reaching fingers of green. The helix flattens into a long, slow glide as the beast begins its approach to the region of light.

Kishimo is conscious of the water passing in and out of her lungs like air. The temperature has risen. The tumbling blocks of ice have grown fewer and smaller and finally have disappeared. The reaching green fronds have become thicker and more luxuriant, varying in their shade and their configuration. The glowing region beneath the fronds stands revealed as earth, as a white sandy soil.

A gasp escapes the lips of Kishimo and she is surprised to hear her voice clearly, strongly. She exclaims, *Oh!*

The Aizen turns and peers at her over one shoulder, his face framed by the *hoshi*-studded helmet with its dragon decoration. He does not speak, but nods, smiling oddly to Kishimo.

The beast glides over waving, weaving plants as tall and as thick as great trees; circles slowly, drifting lower, lower until a clear area appears among the plants. Kishimo peers downward, astonished to see what appears as a pond within the clearing.

If they are moving through water, if the site beneath them is in fact sea bottom and the great weaving growths are marine vegetation—how can there be a pond? Waters beneath the waters? A lake at the bottom of the sea?

Kishimo restrains her puzzlement, waiting for the inevitable descent of the mount. As they approach the tops of the waving marine vegetation she sees figures moving near the edge of the pond, moving not as fish but as men—or as something rather like men.

The beast drifts still lower. The creatures clustered near the pond look up and point. Kishimo watches them; she sees that they are not men such as she has seen before—nor creatures of any sort known to her: *kappa, shikome.*

They are utterly without hair—why this should strike the Kishimo before all else she herself does not understand. Their form is like that of men but their skin is smooth, scaly, like that of fish. The color of it is a pale green-blue. Their eyes are huge, flat, fish-like, with small noses and broad-lipped mouths full of sharp, glittering teeth.

As they breathe she sees pink slits open and close, open and close, at the base of their throats.

Strangely, despite their piscoid appearance, they are apparently sexed as humans: men and women, moving without clothing, the organs of both unashamedly exposed, the breasts of the women small but unmistakable, the organs of the men protruding nakedly.

The beast carrying Kishimo and Aizen lowers itself gently to the beach beside the pond. As the beast makes a final pass before landing, it passes over the pond and Kishimo sees it as a dark, heavily dense fluid, opaque and reflective, giving back a perfect, shimmering image of beast and riders.

They pass from over the pond, drop softly onto the beach; the fish-people who had clustered and jabbered and pointed at the flying monster seem to have lost courage at the final moment. They flee. None remains to greet the newcomers.

Aizen dismounts, turns to Kishimo, and extends his armored

hand in a strange gesture of courtesy. Amused at the inapropos ceremony, she accepts the hand and drops lightly to the ground. To her slippered feet it has the feel of sand: dry, warm, grainy. She finds it difficult to retain her belief that they are deep beneath the Sea of Mists, that above them stretch leagues of salt water, that great cubes and jagged chunks of ice tumble and drift through these waters, that somewhere above a storm may well continue to rage, buffeting both the battle-torn ship *Ofuna* and the ice-clogged black raider.

Where are we now? Kishimo asks the Aizen.

Where the beast has set us down, he replies.

She turns to survey the beast and observes that it has wandered away, wings folded to its sides, legs picking their way daintily over sand and occasional rocks and between plants.

We are still beneath the sea? Kishimo asks. This is all—sweeps a hand through the surrounding—water?

That, yes, Aizen nods.

And the creatures that ran? Kishimo persists.

Aizen frowns. These are the people of this place. I hold no authority over them. But perhaps they will help us.

Kishimo grins. Help us to do what?

The Aizen shrugs. Would you live here forever? That we could do. We could dine on fish and sea plants. Perhaps we could learn the nature of the stuff in the pond. He gestures. But would you stay here forever, Kishimo?

She shakes her head. No, Lord Aizen. No.

Well then. We must find the people of this place. I will talk to their king. We will make our way to the land of Tsunu. The Miroku must not be disappointed.

No, Kishimo agrees, the Miroku must not be disappointed.

The Aizen walks in a small circle, finds the direction in which the fish-men disappeared. He draws his *tachi,* his longsword, and holds it hilt downward before him. He begins to walk forward, is joined by Kishimo.

The light comes from the sands beneath their feet. Kishimo steals a glance upward before they pass between ranks of tall swaying sea vegetation. There is no sky as she has known sky;

no blue dome, no starry black canopy, no gray cloud-scurrying plain overhead. There is only water above, marine turtle, chelated arachnid, tiny mollusk, or giant flapping ray. The passage of the swimmers above and about Kishimo and Aizen is uncanny.

But now great leaning plants loom overhead, feathery fronds and rubbery-textured, fat branches swaying and waving in each vagrant current. Kishimo feels no longer the surrounding water as an impediment: she feels as free as if she were surrounded by air only; and yet buoyed, lightened, wafted so that each step is a flight. She peers between the boles of the great marine plants and sees shapes flitting and gliding away, always at the edge of her vision: enemies waiting in ambush, friends prepared to guard and to assist, curious strangers peering and gaping, wild creatures attendant upon business of their own and utterly unconcerned with these strange intruders.

The Aizen remains silent, his longsword held before him like a talisman, his pace purposeful and steady. Kishimo keeps her place at his side, matching long stride for stride.

The pale sand becomes a hard-pounded path, then— strangeness piled upon strangeness—the path gives way to a broad road paved with grandiose irregular blocks of carven stone, stone fitted so carefully that no space remains between blocks but only the faintest of cracks indicating where one piece of stone ends and another begins.

And the carven stones are crafted to represent grotesque beings, strange deeds, peculiar symbols.

The Aizen ignores the carvings. The woman Kishimo has barely time to glance at them as her feet skip over their hard surface.

For before them rises the most startling sight of all: tall and majestic, its towers soaring in grace and glory, a shimmering city made all of crystal and gold!

8

The surrounding growth draws back almost as if in conscious deference to the approaching city. The road of carven stones grows more wide as the man-god and the woman draw near to the city. For the distance of a bowshot around the city walls there is no life, only the dry white sand and harsh jagged rocks.

Aizen and Kishimo emerge from the forest and stand facing the city wall across a stretch of raw ground. Kishimo watches Aizen as he hails the city: he places hands to mouth and calls. A guard atop the wall responds, waves a *sashimono* bearing the crest of the city, its *mon*. Then the *sashimono,* the small flag, is withdrawn.

Together Kishimo and the Aizen advance to the city wall. From the edge of the forest it appeared low, the towers of the city rearing well above its crest. As they reach the base of the wall, however, Kishimo realizes that it is tall, as tall as the highest mast of *Ofuna*.

Kishimo gazes upward at the city wall. Her sight, drawn upward, continues to rise. High above, where sky should be, is the strange sight of passing sea snakes, skates, turtles, fish. Beyond these is a gray glittering sheet. *Ah,* Kishimo's thought exclaims, *this is the top of the sea*. The glittering sheet is in truth the choppy face of the Sea of Mists, and beyond it is the true air, the true sky, the world from which she came.

From the city come the rattle of chains, the boom of timbers, the creak of hinges not often called upon to move. The great gates of the city tremble. Kishimo waits to see them creep outward, but instead a small door, so cleverly worked into the pattern of the greater ones that she has not seen it until now, creaks inward upon itself.

In it stands the guardian of the gate in full armor and bearing a barb-tipped pike. He is, of course, one of the fish-people Kishimo saw beside the pool in the forest, but here he does not stand naked. His garb is complete and correct, although in making and design distinctly strange.

He bows formally and demands the rights of the visitors.

Aizen bows, Kishimo bows. Aizen speaks: he identifies himself and Kishimo by name, states that they seek the hospitality of the city and its king, his aid in continuing the journey that will bring them, in time, to the land of Tsunu.

The guardian stands aside and bows Aizen and Kishimo into the city. Within the gate watch other guardians, all in helmet, cuirass, kimono and breeches, armor. All carrying pikes with barbed heads or with long curving *naginata* blades.

The door screeches shut behind Kishimo and Aizen. They are escorted courteously by pike-carrying guardians through the streets of the city, past splendid dwellings, well-tended gardens, shimmering ponds, eating houses, workshops. Kishimo sees the citizens of the place as they go about their business, carrying goods, sees their children at play. These are all fish-people, of course.

At length Kishimo and Aizen, with their guides, approach the palace and halt at a new wall, this one decorated with imperial emblems, stylized flowers, and graceful characters. Rows of *sashimono* wave from staffs atop the palace wall, proclaiming the families of the court of the city.

The guardians escorting Kishimo and Aizen hail the palace retainers and again gates swing wide; Kishimo and Aizen advance onto the palace grounds and the guardians fall away, leaving them in the tutelage of the palace retainers.

These are fish-men of another sort than Kishimo has seen before. All are tall, broad of shoulder, stern of countenance. The helmets worn by them are of the *eboshi-nara* type with *oni* crest, the crest shaped like a fierce one-horned demon, the helmet formed of metal to resemble a tall court cap. The leader of the retainers wears also a *so-men,* armored mask of metal, with holes for eyes, nostrils, mouth. Instead of pike, bow, or sword, these retainers carry *sode-garami,* sleeve entanglers, long sticks fitted with cross-bars and many sharp teeth for catching intruders and unruly guests upon the woven cloth of their kimonos.

There is much bowing between the Aizen and Kishimo on the one side and the palace retainers on the other.

At length the retainers lead the guests through gorgeous gardens of carefully tended marine vegetation separated by paths of patterned gravel in many colors, alternating stripes of gray, maroon, white, beige. Ornate cages taller than a mounted warrior stand within the gardens. Within these swim creatures on exhibition: graceful goldfish with great round eyes and waving fins as soft and thin as finest silk; giant *heike* crabs with the faces of fallen warriors graven on the backs of their shells; squids pacing restlessly to and fro, propelling themselves with jets of water, long tentacles trailing behind as they move.

At the entrance to the palace itself, Kishimo and Aizen are turned over to yet another group of retainers and ushered within. They are led to the court chamber and presented to the king of the city.

They bow low before the king.

He bids them rise and take seats upon cushions; courtiers bring sweetmeats for them to nibble, fish-women as skillful as geishas bring tea and pour it into tiny cups for all to drink.

When everyone is refreshed, the king instructs his guests to justify their presence in his city. Kishimo's companion rises and bows, tells the king that he himself is the Aizen, intent upon conquest of the land of Tsunu, trapped by *kappa* and frozen on board the raider ship in the battle with Miroku's craft *Ofuna,* freed by the intervention of Kishimo and the power of her life-flame, lost beneath the Sea of Mists, and only by accident present in the realm of the king.

The king listens carefully, saying not a word until the Aizen has finished. He watches the Aizen bow low once more; the king signs him to return to his cushion. He turns his regal countenance toward Kishimo, demands to know her identity and her business.

She gives her name. She states that she remembers another realm, another mode of being from which she was brought by the Aizen. But she does not recall the time before that, only vague recollections of a place of vast emptiness and swirling clouds of inchoate matter. Now she knows only that the Miroku told her who she is, that she is the ally of the Miroku and the Aizen equally while their truce persists. That in the end she does not know her purpose or her destiny.

Ah! the king exclaims. He asks if his visitors wish to know where they are and who he is.

Politely the Aizen and Kishimo indicate such a wish.

You have found your way to Yomi, the king tells them. The Land of Gloom. Here all things persist forever although elsewhere time continues to revolve. I am master of this city, Ryujin, known to some as the Dragon King of the Sea. The people of Yomi are sailors and travelers lost at sea. Their loved ones in the world above wait and wait for their return, but people of Yomi never return to the land above. They are not sorry here, nor happy. They are not impatient. They live as if in the world above but they do not age, alter, nor die. Children remain children forever; old men and women remain forever old, never dying, nor are children born in the Land of Gloom.

Aizen rises angrily. We cannot remain here, he exclaims. Should the Miroku reach the land of Tsunu and be defeated, all will be lost. Should he conquer Tsunu, all the worse for Aizen! Ryujin the King of the Sea must free the travelers to continue on their journey!

The king listens, smiling slowly, stroking his chin. From the chin of Ryujin grows a small beard, white and wispy, looking like the silky tail fin of a giant goldfish. The king runs long thin fingers through his beard, beaming. You are my guests, he proclaims. You will remain in Yomi at my pleasure. If you wish to depart, you must win your way away from Yomi.

How? the Aizen demands.

Ah, the king replies, all in good time. Now you will retire and prepare yourselves for our court ceremonies. He claps his hands and functionaries attend upon him and his guests. Kishimo and Aizen are ushered from the presence of King Ryujin. Kishimo wishes to ask Aizen many questions but she says nothing in the presence of court functionaries. They carry sleeve entanglers, *sode-garami,* but treat the Kishimo and the Aizen with deference and respect.

They are shown to sumptuous quarters and attendants take their dirty clothing, usher them to hot baths, wash them, offer fresh raiment, provide them with court regalia, offer them couches upon which to recline.

A chamberlain arrives and instructs them both in the etiquette of Ryujin's court, a court unlike others.

At length the chamberlain asks if they are duly rested or if they wish to sleep before returning for court ceremony. Kishimo and Aizen indicate that they are ready to return to Ryujin's presence. The chamberlain bows, thanks them, claps his hands. An assistant arrives bearing court caps and *tachi* to replace the scarred weapons of the sea battle, the *hoshi-kabuto* of Aizen, and the *han-buri* worn by Kishimo.

Aizen has been outfitted with blue-silk-bound cuirass, *midori-fukaki-odoshi no mogami-do,* and court cap. His figure is splendid, his appearance proud, in court regalia.

Kishimo wears no armor but silken-decorated kimono draped gracefully, broad colorful *obi,* silken *hakama* breeches, split-toe socks, and straw sandals. Her feeling of self is cool and in no means uneasy.

The chamberlain leads them through palace corridors, at length returning to the court of King Ryujin. The court is no longer in session in the small audience chamber where the king greeted them earlier; now they enter a great room decorated with *sashimono,* small flags, and *kakemono,* painted scrolls of heroes, gods, battles, supernatural beings.

Musicians play upon flutes, drums, *baiwa, koto.*

Illusionists and magicians stroll to and fro, entertaining

members of the court with clever entertainments, making small goldfish appear and disappear, causing fires to spring up in the midst of their wonderment, bringing the faces of mortals into being and then sending them back to their world above, perhaps to tell friends that they have had a vision or a dream.

Trained rays sweep into the room, pressing the water with their finny wings as if they were birds in the air. To the accompaniment of *koto* and flute they loop and circle like dancers, their barbed tails raised high behind them, venom held away from courtiers, each gracious sweep of wing and tilt of body attuned to a note or chord.

Ryujin the king smiles, gestures with his fan.

A court chamberlain rewards the trainer of the rays with pearls and coins drawn from a treasure chest, the tribute of some argosy long since crumpled on rocks or battered by wind and wave and sunken to the Land of Gloom, to Yomi, the domain of Ryujin.

Court attendants appear, serving heated jugs of rice wine with tiny porcelain cups for all. Kishimo accepts a cup from a bowing attendant. She is seated beside Aizen on a silken cushion embroidered with patterns of willows.

King Ryujin holds his *sake* cup aloft. There is silence in the room; musicians, courtesans, nobles, guests, attendants, entertainers alike attend to the king. He downs his cup of *sake.* All others follow suit. Ryujin gestures with his fan to the majordomo. The majordomo claps his hands and the orchestra strikes up a thrilling tune. From behind a screen to the Dragon King's left emerges a samurai dressed all in blue and black with armor tied in blue silk and lamellae of blue-black alloy.

From behind a screen to the Dragon King's right emerges a samurai dressed all in red and gold with armor tied in flame-red silk and lamellae of red-yellow alloy.

The samurai advance to stand before the Dragon King, bow to him, receive acknowledgment with a flick of the royal fan, rise and turn, bow to each other.

Each is armed with *daisho,* paired swords: *tachi,* longsword, and *tanto,* shortsword with armor-piercing blade. The red samurai wears a red-yellow alloy *o-boshi,* great star-shaped helmet. The blue samurai wears an unusual *namban-kabuto,* a tall helmet of the type once favored by northern barbarians with a stylized carp for its decoration.

Both draw *tachi,* longswords. The swords bear lengthy hilts, enameled and inlaid with significant designs. The blue-black alloy sword hilt is decorated with mother-of-pearl in patterns of willows, chrysanthemums, bushes. The flame-red hilt is decorated with gold inlays of dragons. The *tsuba,* sword guards, are similarly decorated: with flowers, with dragons.

The samurai present their *tachi.* They gesture and feint, circling each other on the polished marble floor before the royal throne. The Dragon King Ryujin watches, royal fan held tightly, eyes fixed on maneuvering samurai.

The red samurai slashes two-handed at his rival: he sweeps his *tachi* above his head, shouts—*Ai!*—and swings. Light glistens on his blade.

The blue samurai parries, raising his *tachi* to catch the blow on the top of his blade, permitting it to slide harmlessly along the blade and bound away from the willow-decorated *tsuba.* He leaps backward. The *tachi* of the red samurai sweeps past him and the red samurai leaps in a complete circle, recovering from the unsuccessful blow and planting his feet wide apart, holding his knees bent, *tachi* once more at the ready.

The blue samurai feints an overhead blow, jabs his elbows to the side, and sweeps his *tachi* at the waist of his opponent. The longsword swishes, glinting, beneath the red samurai's still-raised arms and sword.

Uh! the red samurai grunts, and jerks backward to avoid the blow. The *tachi* of the blue samurai glances from the cuirass of the red; flame-colored silken cords are slit and dangle loosely; the red samurai grunts again, *Uh!*

The blue samurai shouts a syllable of exaltation. *Ai!* He follows up his blow, continuing in a circle, sweeping his sword upward and bringing it down in a two-handed sweep at the head of the red. The blade strikes the *o-boshi kabuto,* the great star-shaped helmet of yellow-red alloy. The sound of its contact rings through the court chamber.

The Dragon King Ryujin indicates his approval of the skillful blow with a gesture of his fan.

The red samurai, although his helmet has saved him from the direct effects of the blow, is staggered by its impact. His face appears blank, his fingers flex and stiffen. The dragon-inlaid sword hilt drops from his *yugake*-covered fingers and clatters onto the marble floor.

The blue samurai kicks his opponent's *tachi* aside with a single jab of one armored foot. The sword skids across the polished marble and is retrieved by a chamberlain, placed carefully upon a red and yellow *katanakake,* a decorated sword stand covered with dragon symbols to match the motif of the samurai and his armament.

The blue samurai advances to administer a coup de grace to his opponent but the red is not finished. Even in his half daze he staggers away from the blue, permitting no opportunity for the other to strike the final blow. The blue samurai stalks his opponent, not hastily. Sword raised, blue-black chrysanthemum-decorated hilt grasped in *yugake* gloves, he prepares to finish his rival.

But the red samurai recovers his wits sufficiently to grope in his *obi,* find the scabbard of his *tanto* shortsword.

From her cushion beside that of the Aizen, Kishimo observes the scabbard: it is of lacquered and polished *same,* the skin of a ray. The hilt of the shortsword is like that of the red samurai's *tachi,* decorated with figures of dragons. The blade itself, as the warrior draws it, shows relief figures of dragon motif.

The red samurai halts.

The blue stands facing him, raises his *tachi* once again to administer the final, the fatal, blow. Blood can be seen now, seeping from beneath the cuirass of the red samurai, floating gracefully in the water of the court chamber.

The blue samurai begins the downward sweep of his longsword but as he does so the red warrior charges audaciously forward, *tanto* held unconventionally before him, its armor-piercing blade directed at the cuirass-protected belly of the blue samurai.

The red samurai strikes first; his blade, driven with the strength of both arms and the weight of his forward charge, slides somehow between lamellar plates of the blue warrior. There is a hesitation less lengthy than the intake of a gasp of astonishment and the blade pierces the *do-maru* cuirass of the blue samurai.

A great gout of blood spurts from the wound and obscures the pale water between the two fighters.

But the overhead blow of the blue samurai is already in motion and the awful wound to the fighter does not stay its delivery. Once more the *tachi* is aimed at the *kabuto* of the opponent, but at the wound to the belly of the blue samurai his flashing *tachi* slides aside, then curves back, striking the red samurai at the base of the neck where helmet and cuirass meet. The blade strikes as if aimed with an eagle eye. Its razor-like edge slices inward and downward, half severing the head of its target.

Another shower of blood wells upward into the clear water.

Curious fish from higher levels, responding to the sudden access of blood, come nosing about the court and are shooed away by chamberlains and retainers.

The two samurai fall side by side before the throne of the Dragon King Ryujin.

The ruler indicates his pleasure with a gesture of the royal fan and a loud, slowly expelled hiss. The court follow suit.

Chamberlains remove the bodies of the two warriors.

Kishimo expresses her surprise at the fatal entertainment until a court functionary crouches beside her cushion, bows, softly explains that the two samurai will be carried to a place of safety and honor, that by the morrow their fatal wounds will be healed and that they will then return to court proceedings, to participate in entertainment at the pleasure of Ryujin.

Once more *sake* is passed, this time with rice cakes for nibbling. The blood of the samurai clears slowly, the curious fish proceed about their business, and the court moves to its next order of entertainment, a wrestling match between two nearly naked *sumo.*

Kishimo sips at her hot rice wine, nibbles at cakes, and wonders what fate lies in store for herself and her companion the Aizen.

At length the entertainment is completed and members of the court bow and withdraw until only Ryujin the king, Kishimo, Aizen, and a single chamberlain remain.

You were entertained, I hope, by the ceremonies and proceedings of my court, the king declaims.

Together Aizen and Kishimo express their pleasure and gratitude. The Aizen offers to repay the royal hospitality in whatever way he may. He is a man-god; his abilities may be of use or of pleasure to the Dragon King.

No, Ryujin says, we take pleasure in the Land of Gloom to give hospitality to travelers, for so few of them pass. But what would you of us? the Dragon King asks.

We still seek our way to the land of Tsunu.

Ryujin turns toward his chamberlain. The guests may climb to the peak of this tower, the king states.

The chamberlain bows.

King Ryujin rises.

Kishimo and Aizen bow.

King Ryujin bows and departs.

The chamberlain signs Kishimo and Aizen to follow him as he exits the court chamber. Have you other belongings? he asks. Are you prepared to depart?

Kishimo and Aizen wear court-provided clothing, carry the armor and the weapons with which they are provided. They will be permitted to travel with whatever they wish. From within his kimono the chamberlain draws two jewels and presents them to Kishimo and Aizen. These, he says, are the Nanjiu and the Kanjiu jewels. The chamberlain holds them high. Their flash fills the chamber. These are saved for other visitors yet to come, he says. But I will lend them to you. They are the jewels of the tides of the sea.

The Nanjiu is the jewel of the rising tide, the chamberlain explains. The Kanjiu is the jewel of the ebbing tide. You need merely hold the jewel of the rising tide to your forehead and command the waters to rise, and wherever you are, be it by the shore or at the tallest mountain peak, the waves will come rolling to you. To dispense with the waters, use the jewel of the ebbing tide. Hold it to your brow, command the waters to fall, and fall they shall.

He holds out the two jewels to the Aizen and the Kishimo, their facets flashing, Nanjiu, Kanjiu, brilliant colors, through all the regal chamber.

The Aizen reaches for the jewels with both his hands but Kishimo places one hand upon the sleeve of the chamberlain before he has placed the jewels in the hands of the Aizen. The chamberlain grins knowingly and places one sparkling jewel in the extended *yugake* of Aizen, the other in that of Kishimo.

They stride together from the court chamber and stand in the garden of the palace. Kishimo places the jewel she has received against her forehead and silently commands the sea to recede. The gem gleams with blinding glory. The water draws back from about the Kishimo, leaving her in an airy dome here in the Land of Gloom.

After a moment Aizen raises Nanjiu to his brow and shortly the waters return.

All smile at one another.

Come, says the chamberlain, accompany me to the highest tower of the palace. He turns and begins to climb a flight built upon the outer face of the tall palace. Aizen follows him, and Kishimo follows the Aizen.

9

Thus proceeding to climb the flight that surrounds the palace, the three fall into the telling of tales. The Aizen, whose tale at the court of Ryujin the Dragon King had been sparse and reluctantly narrated, waxes eloquent, revealing more of his nature and history than he has previously chosen to do.

In the realm of the gods whence Aizen arose, his full name was Aizen-myu, a name meaning, simply, Love. In the higher realm he was a very different being from the one he is in the half-worlds of the Sea of Mists and the Land of Gloom. In the higher realm of the gods he had been the god of passion; his body had had eight arms and was provided with bow and arrow for smiting love into the hearts of mortals.

But he had struggled against passion. In the midst of his bristling hair a lion had appeared. He had set a foot on the path of the desire for enlightenment; his passion had been sublimated into this search.

He had traveled from the realm of the gods to the half-world, here to pursue the path of enlightenment. When the high goal was achieved he might return to the upper realm.

Is this how you seek enlightenment? asks the chamberlain. Does one achieve enlightenment by the pursuit of rivalry and of conquest?

Aizen frowns. One seeks enlightenment anywhere, he replies. One brings about justice, the correction of wrongs. One can attain enlightenment through the performance of good works as well as through the study of scripture or the contemplation of puzzles.

When Aizen completes his recitation, silence descends upon the three and they climb thus for many hundreds of paces. The Kishimo peers downward over the course they have already covered and is unable longer to see the palace, the courtyard and garden, the road they had traversed, the forest of marine trees. She peers above and sees only the canopy of the sea. Night must have fallen in the upper world, for the canopy is black, and only the faintest of rays such as those thrown down by the moon and stars penetrate the water.

After a long time Kishimo reiterates her story, as she had told it at court. With one hand she feels the jewel Kanjiu safely tucked with her *obi*. Then with her hand she feels the thumping of the heart within her bosom. She tells her companions that she may have had her origin in the primal realm, before even the reed-deity had arisen, long before Izanami and Izanagi had strode out upon the *ama no uki hashi,* the floating bridge of heaven, there to disturb the oily waters and stir up the island Onogoro.

Who can tell what realms exist? Kishimo asks wistfully. What realms of beings? What worlds of worlds? What strange seas, what wondrous lands, what races of gods and men and beasts? Who knows what realms I passed through before by chance encountering the Aizen? In time I shall reach my goal, such as it is, and then shall I know the purpose of my journey, be it to assist Miroku in regaining the land of Tsunu or some other end. For now I pursue that path which is opened to me, learning and seeking what may be found.

As Kishimo finishes her tale, silence falls upon the three once more. The canopy begins to grow brighter. The three continue to climb and to stare at fish that approach to examine them with diffidence and with curiosity.

At last the chamberlain suggests that they halt their climbing for a while. They reach a kind of platform or landing along the path of their ascent, an area of flat expanse, sandy surface, with the jagged wall of the palace tower, gold and glass made into the form of mountain crags, on one side and water depths on the other. Here one could simply step off the landing and drift downward through the sea to return to the Land of Gloom, Yomi, and to the court of the Dragon King Ryujin, with one more tale of adventure to tell.

Instead, the chamberlain builds a small fire, calling upon Kishimo to use the jewel of the ebbing tide to make a dome of air for them over the landing. Driftwood is piled and flint is struck to make flame. The chamberlain brings sweetmeats and *sake* from beneath his kimono and they feast on light meal and drink delicate cups of *sake* until they are happy and refreshed.

The chamberlain says, You have graciously told me your tales and made no demand in return. I will give you my own story. My name is Susano-wu. My house is of the oldest in the kingdom of Yomi. My people were people of the sea longer than any others save the dynasty of the Dragon Kings themselves. We were connected by blood with the dynasty of kings, and held positions of the highest honor at the court of the Dragon Kings and throughout the Land of Gloom for many generations.

The symbol and honor of my house was a sword, the sword Kuzanagi, a blade of great honor and magical power, which was wrested from an ancestor by a dragon or serpent of wondrous make. The thing possessed eight heads, each with a different voice, each with a different face. The serpent won the blade Kuzanagi from my kinsman, and in disgrace our house was lowered to the rank of court chamberlain in the service of the Dragon King dynasty. Ever since have we served the Dragon Kings of the Land of Gloom.

Susano-wu falls silent, tends fire, distributes rice cakes to the others, who nibble at them, awaiting the speaker's resumption. But Susano-wu remains silent.

Ah, says Aizen at last, and *Ah,* says Kishimo.

Do you return to Yomi and the court of Ryujin after escorting us to the upper realm? Kishimo asks the question of Susano-wu.

There is silence once again, filled only with the soft and pleasant crackle of the driftwood fire. The odor of black and orange embers billows upward and upon reaching the limit of the dome of air given by the Kanjiu jewel makes tiny bubbles; these, too, continue upward, shimmering with reflected red firelight from below.

Susano-wu folds his hands, an expression of strain crossing his face. He possesses a long mustache that droops at either corner of his mouth. Both his mustache and his eyebrows are pure black in color and glossy and soft in appearance. At length he speaks to the others:

If you will so permit (Susano-wu pleads) I would join you in your journey. In the Land of Gloom, Yomi, I think I would live very long without opportunity to recoup the honor of my family. So (he shrugs eloquently) my service, and the service of my line to follow, would fail to discharge our punishment. Years or generations hence, my house would still be one of chamberlains.

The Aizen asks, Is that not an honorable station?

Susano-wu smiles wistfully. To the common peasant, a chamberlain at the court of the Dragon King is one exalted. Ah, but to one whose ancestors were the cronies and the chief advisers of those same kings, the comedown is disgrace. I think (Susano-wu halts and waves a long-fingered hand expressively) that my ancestor would better have satisfied honor by offering the act of *hara-kiri.*

But, for whatever reason, he failed even in that. Thus I bear the double disgrace. One cannot expiate the shame of another, of course, by the noble act of *hara-kiri.* But if I could encounter the serpent and defeat it, if I could regain the sword Kuzanagi from the dragon, then the dishonor would be erased and my family would be restored to its former place of esteem.

To Kishimo's surprise, Aizen glances at her. She reads in his eyes a question, a search for assent. The Aizen actually consulting her before making his reply to the chamberlain Susano-wu!

Kishimo nods to Aizen. She raises one hand and presses the flesh of it against her chest.

Aizen invites Susano-wu to join their party and continue

beyond the surface of the Sea of Mists into the upper realm, there with Aizen and Kishimo to seek out, if he can, the serpent and regain the lost sword Kuzanagi.

Susano-wu bows his head, expressing gratitude. He clears the remains of the fire, makes clean the flat place where the three have rested. All rise and prepare to continue on their way.

The Aizen raises to his forehead the Nanjiu jewel, commands the waters to return; the dome of air rushes upward as a single shimmering ball and disappears overhead. The prospect ahead of the three is more rising stairs, more glass and gold formed as jagged mountain. The canopy remains black.

They climb without fatigue but also without speech. There is little light, and in the watery gloom grotesque fish dangling lanterns pass silently, seeking out their meals. Without warning, the head and shoulders of Susano-wu, who walks in the lead, disappear as if cut off by a great blade sweeping across his form. Kishimo is momentarily startled but Susano-wu continues to ascend, the visible remainder of his form growing shorter with each stride.

Follows Aizen: the dragon-crested helmet, neck guard, cuirass, leg armor, foot armor disappear through the roof of the watery realm. As his trailing *kogake* foot armor is drawn through the surface there remains only a circle of ripples spreading across the roof above Kishimo's head.

She draws her lungs full of water and steps forward and upward, breaking through the surface. Cascades of black water tumble about her ears, washing her hair down upon her shoulders, her bosom, and her back. She continues to rise, shaking back her hair, shifting it with her hands so that it lies wholly upon her back, away from her face. With a final stride Kishimo pulls herself totally from the grasp of the sea.

She blows out the contents of her mouth, lungs, nose, the water streaming down her body and back to return to its own world as if eager to avoid airy entrapment. Kishimo draws her first breath of air since leaving the upper realm. Cold and jagged, it tears her lungs; yet the sensation is as pleasurable as it is painful. She exhales, draws in deeper breath, heaving her lungs full, shoving her shoulders back as far as she can, throwing her head back so that her face points upward to the black sky.

There are stars scattered widely across the heavens, bright points gleaming white, red, green. Suddenly—and startlingly—Kishimo is overcome with joy and relief. Why the sight of these glittering motes should bring about such a reaction she does not know, but her eyes fill with tears, hot wetness contrasting with the clinging chill of the lower realm. She feels the tears running along the planes of her face, great bursting sobs of air punching in and out of her lungs. Her heart pounds, pounds, she cannot tell whether hotly or coldly.

To her astonishment, the Aizen turns toward her. He is taller than she and far more broadly made. He circles her shoulders with his heavy arms and draws her to him. Her cheek rests against his chest, the silk-tied ribbing of his cuirass absorbing her hot spilled tears. The thought of this strikes her as amusing and she shakes once with a short laugh made up still of half a sob. How has the almost skeletal Aizen changed to this bulky form?

She turns her face upward to his and he looks at her, an unreadable expression on his lips and about his eyes.

Kishimo expresses thanks to the Aizen and he drops his arms from about her. He steps back and Kishimo looks around. They are standing on a shore: black, sharply ridged rocks rising through a thin layer of sand. Inland from the narrow beach, rocky cliffs rise, silhouetted against the sky. Beyond them Kishimo can perceive the tops of trees.

Away from the land, water extends to the horizon. It is black and featureless save for the luminous lines of foam thrown against sand and rocks where low swells tumble and break under a fresh onshore breeze. The breeze is strangely warm and carries pleasant, unidentifiable scents upon it.

Far off where black sea and black sky unite there is a faint suggestion of lightening. Here will rise the sun after a little time.

We have reached the upper realm, Susano-wu says. We have set our feet upon a path which cannot now be reversed.

The Aizen challenges: Can we not return to Yomi?

Susano-wu chuckles coldly. As others have reached the Land of Gloom, so may we. Sailors lost in the Sea of Mists find their way to Yomi. Pirates and their victims, killed at sea, do the same. And so may we.

Aizen glares angrily at Susano-wu. He turns then toward Kishimo. Without his speaking she understands his wish. She raises the Kanjiu jewel to her brow and commands the waters to recede. The water at their feet, its many tongues lapping quietly at the white sand and black rock of the shore, pulls back to reveal—more white sand and black rock, shreds of seaweed, sticks of driftwood, a few scurrying crabs, a couple of flopping white-bellied fish.

Susano-wu grins defiantly. You thought to see the tower of the palace of the Dragon Kings. But all you see is the floor of these waters, the edge of the Sea of Mists. You will not find your way back to Yomi thus.

Aizen lifts the Nanjiu jewel to his own brow, pressing it beneath the helm of his dragon-crested *kabuto,* and commands the waters to return. In the space of a breath the gently lapping wavelets have returned to their former level, purling and foaming about the feet of Susano-wu, Kishimo, Aizen. He lowers the jewel, places it in a fold of his kimono inside the silk-cord-bound cuirass of his armor.

Aizen places the fist of one armored hand against the plated hip guard of his armor; the other, on the decorated hilt of his lacquer-handled longsword. He turns in a complete circle, searching shadowed cliffs, rocky beach, wave-chopped black sea, and dim sky with eyes peering from beneath the hard edge of his helmet. Then he murmurs softly, What will you now, Susano-wu? How will you regain the sword Kuzanagi and the honor of your family?

With great gravity edged with a suggestion of mockery Susano-wu responds. Perhaps my foe will greet me upon this very stand, Lord Aizen. But I will not await the serpent here. Rather will I pursue the enemy and seek the sword Kuzanagi. I see no chance of profit in waiting here, in strolling the beach or wading to sea. Hence would I search inland and trust to encounter what or who may be of interest to me.

Aizen nods in agreement but does not move until Susano-wu strides to the base of the rocky bluff overtowering the beach. Carefully he begins to climb, selecting handhold and foothold with care, making each move with great strength and assurance. Aizen glances at the Kishimo and she feels a rare sense of communication and communion with him. Without speaking they agree to proceed with Susano-wu, up the rocky cliff, to find what lies above the beach and beyond the wall.

Kishimo climbs, black rock before her face, sand beneath her feet, sea lapping softly at the beach behind her. The sky shows a flush of approaching dawn but overhead it remains dark enough to contrast with the gleam and wink of stars. Although clad only in kimono, breeches, slippers, and gloves, Kishimo is armed. Yet she now finds that the absence of helmet, cuirass, shoulder and leg and hand armor leaves her more agile and hence better able to climb the rock wall than either Aizen or Susano-wu. Her breath comes steadily, evenly, despite the effort of climbing. Her muscles are strong, relaxed; she is filled with energy and a strange joy at the activity of climbing.

She reaches the edge of the bluff and reaches a rough overhang of scrubby grass onto the flat surface above; before exerting the effort to pull herself onto the flatness, she shifts about, sees Aizen and Susano-wu struggling and gasping in her wake. Her eyes narrow, rise from the crab-like figures of the males, sweep the choppy sea to gray-on-gray horizon.

As if to her cue there is a flash of gold and red. Clouds drifting high above the water explode with colors: purple, rose, vermillion, scarlet, tangerine, chrome, white. Rays flash from beneath the horizon as if mighty torches were blasting the tints through the sea. Flames writhe and curl: the sun, the Mirror of Amaterasu, springs out of the choppy grim sea and sprays the universe with brilliance and life.

Kishimo recoils from the sudden brilliance, whirls to see the form of a woman's head and shoulders marked in deep black against the now light-drenched gray rock wall: her own shadow outlined in dawnlight.

A cry of life and joy bursts unsummoned from her lips. She gulps her full intake of morning air, suddenly aware of the taste and satisfaction in it. She flexes the muscles of her arms and draws herself across the edge of the bluff; raising one knee to her chest, she springs erect, whirls to face the rising sun, feels with her slippered feet the grassy earth as a lover grasps the flesh of a lover, looks into the brilliant, distant sun, raises both arms in exultation, shouts a single syllable of praise and welcome to the Mirror.

One, then two black dots rise above the edge of the cliff. A tiny dragon, metallic, the sun glinting from behind it, its eyes like tiny glowing jewels in the still dawn. A helmet. A hand. A man: the Aizen.

Another: Susano-wu.

Kishimo turns her back on them to survey the inland reaches that lie ahead.

Facing her is a figure as tall as a young palm, armored in heavy iron plates of the antique *tanko* variety, armed with round shield and longsword, standing with feet spread, shield on arm, sword in hand. The sun pouring its rays from behind Kishimo lights the figure brightly, setting it off against the backdrop of grassy plain and lush trees.

Only the face of the figure is obscure. Kishimo narrows her eyes, peers into the space beneath the helm of the stranger, is unable to see more than darkness there and the vague suggestion of a male face, eyes glowing small and deepset within smoky darkness.

At a sound from behind her Kishimo turns her head and glances over her shoulder toward the sea. Aizen and Susano-wu have reached the edge of the bluff and drawn themselves upon the flat plain where Kishimo and the stranger confront each other, neither of them having uttered a syllable.

To Kishimo's surprise, first Susano-wu, then Aizen the

man-god, drops to his knees facing the dark figure. Kishimo hears Susano-wu's exclamation: The Spirit Master.

It is indeed the Spirit Master: Okinu-nushi.

Kishimo turns her face toward him once more, toward Okinu-nushi, the Spirit Master. She does not kneel.

10

Nor does the Spirit Master Okinu-nushi speak or move. Kishimo
stands with the sun, the Mirror of Amaterasu, directly behind
her, its early rays glinting off the choppy surface of the dark Sea
of Mists; yet the sky and air are very clear. Perhaps this island
at the edge of the Sea of Mists, where the eternal fogs and
storms of that cold, moist region hiss and scream, marks a
boundary. Perhaps, beyond this point, all is different.

The sun's rays fall fully upon Okinu-nushi; they illuminate his
helmet and his armor, failing only to penetrate the brim of the
iron *kabuto* to show his face. It is a moment of strange stillness
with only the soft lapping of waters against rocky shore to break
the total silence of the morn. Aizen and Susano-wu kneel near
the edge of the bluff, behind Kishimo, while Okinu-nushi stands
facing her, unmoving.

Kishimo hears the air rasping in and out of her lungs, feels its
knife-edge crispness with joy and clarity. She hears the very
blood pounding through her body, her heart thumping in her
chest beneath the thin cloth of her kimono. She gathers her
courage, draws a deep breath of chill air, speaks to the Spirit
Master. But he makes no reply. Kishimo stares at Aizen and
Susano-wu: they remain kneeling, unmoving.

With a single long stride Kishimo advances toward the
Master. The grass beneath her feet is wet with beads of morning
dew and windswept sea spray, beaded and glistening in the
early sunlight. Kishimo walks toward the Spirit Master, one hand

raised involuntarily to press against her bosom. Still Okinu-nushi does not move.

Kishimo halts within a pace of the Spirit Master. She speaks but he does not answer. She raises a hand and moves it as if to touch the Spirit Master upon the ancient-style cuirass that he wears.

As she does so, a jolt of pure frigidity smashes upon her arm and through her body, a cold shudder courses from her outstretched fingers back through all of her form, a wave of intolerable iciness flows from the top of her head to the soles of her feet. Before her eyes, all turns to a pattern of dazzling white, which fades slowly to wintry gray before returning, slowly, to the normal hues of morning, green vegetation, brown soil, black rock, blue heaven.

A tingling fills Kishimo's entire body, emanating from the tips of her fingers that most closely approached Okinu-nushi. She drops her eyes and sees, about the feet of the Spirit Master, a ring of white-frosted grass. About her own feet is a smaller but similar circle of frost. Kishimo exhales and sees that even the air from her lungs hangs frostily in the morning brightness.

So slowly that eyes can barely perceive the motion, the right hand of Okinu-nushi moves. From its position, fist clenched, elbow curved, hand resting upon the hip guard of his *tanko* armor, the fingers deliberately uncurl. The hand slowly rises. The light within the misty eyes beneath the *kabuto* of Okinu-nushi, the light of deepset eyes glowing like coals of fire, grows brighter—yet the face of the Spirit Master becomes no more clear than before.

The Spirit Master draws a breath: a wind fills Kishimo's ears, she is pulled nearly from her feet; scraps of leaf, grass, beads of windspray from the Sea of Mists rush past her. She hears creaking and a thump, thinks of the Aizen and of Susano-wu still kneeling in the grass.

The hand of Okinu-nushi has risen to the height of the Spirit Master's own chest. Now he moves it forward, down, a single finger extended. Kishimo, still recovering from the icy shock of her attempt to touch Okinu-nushi, watches the hand as it approaches her flesh.

The finger touches her once, lightly, then withdraws as gracefully and as deliberately as it approached. A new sensation races through Kishimo's limbs. She feels a rush of flame and of ice at once through her belly, limbs, and head. She stares deeply into the glowing coals of Okinu-nushi's eyes and sees there a message that she understands without the uttering of a word.

The arms of the Spirit Master rise and encircle Kishimo. He turns to face the Aizen and the errant Susano-wu. These kneel yet, their backs to the sea, the wind, the Mirror of Amaterasu. The Spirit Master commands them to state their business in his domain. The two raise their eyes to his; Kishimo sees in the faces of Aizen and Susano-wu awe for the being that towers above them.

On the part of Susano-wu, she can understand this. He is an ordinary mortal—or little more than that. But Aizen? The man-god? The embodiment of passion harnessed to the search for enlightenment? Why does a god bow in awe to the Spirit Master?

Yet Kishimo recalls the Aizen's own statement of his lessened status in the realm of men. Here he is very little different from any ordinary being, little different from Susano-wu. Perhaps he kneels before Okinu-nushi for this reason—or perhaps for some other reason of his own.

Susano-wu speaks, never rising from his knees. He repeats the tale of the sword Kuzanagi and its loss to the serpent, the shame of his family before the court of Yomi. He speaks of Aizen's trek to the land of Tsunu, of Miroku's ship *Ofuna* besieged in the Sea of Mists by the raider; of the battle of Aizen's minions against the *kappa* raiders; of Kishimo's revival of Aizen with the life of her flesh.

Kishimo stands with eyes fixed on Susano-wu as he speaks, feels the arm of Okinu-nushi tighten around her shoulders. At length the Spirit Master demands of Susano-wu that he reveal his wishes.

Spirit Master, Susano-wu says, what will be the path before us, before Aizen, Kishimo, and myself? Where will our quest lead us? What perils will we encounter? Will I regain the sword Kuzanagi? Will the Aizen or the Miroku rule the land of Tsunu in the end?

Okinu-nushi laughs grimly. Kishimo turns her head to look into his face but sees only blackness and the image of smoke curling and drifting from beneath his armor to the visor of his *kabuto,* and the two glowing coals of his eyes gleaming out from within the obscured interior.

In the end.

Okinu-nushi repeats the words: In the end.

Susano-wu says nothing further.

In the end, the Spirit Master says, neither Aizen nor Miroku will rule in the land of Tsunu. In the end they will both find their ways to Yomi. As will you, Susano-wu. As will you. As will *all.*

There is a silence, and the wind sweeps past the ears of Kishimo, carrying the spray from the Sea of Mists onto the iron armor of the Spirit Master.

In the end all perish, Susano-wu says. This, of course, all thinking beings know. But at the end of our quest—will we enjoy success or failure?

For reply there is silence, only the wind from offshore, sweeping a chill salt spray from the wave tops of the Sea of Mists over the coastal bluff, onto and past the four who stand or crouch in the light of morning: Kishimo, Aizen, Susano-wu, Okinu-nushi. Spray accumulates on the *kabuto,* the helmet, of the Spirit Master and beads of water fall from its edge onto the iron cuirass that he wears, running and dropping down his armor and onto the circle of white that surrounds his feet. Here the drops freeze into tiny white stalagmites like a range of fairy mountains standing all around his iron *kogake,* foot armor.

Kishimo hears rustling at her either side and, turning, observes Susano-wu and the Aizen. These have waited, crouched, kneeling, throughout the dialogue; now they have gathered their courage and have risen. Now they approach the Spirit Master, drawing as close as Kishimo, standing one at her left side, one at her right.

Susano-wu says, Spirit Master, we three have passed through the Land of Gloom, Yomi, through the palace of the Dragon King of the Sea, Ryujin.

Perhaps the *kabuto* of Okinu-nushi tips forward as the Spirit Master nods slightly in acknowledgment of the errant's statement.

My powers are as those of any mortal, Susano-wu states.

Again, the iron helmet moves up, moves down—no more than the width of the little finger of a young child.

Aizen, the Aizen-myu, yielded up his heavenly power as well, Susano-wu resumes. This, when he left the upper realm. He is more now than a mortal, but only little.

The iron helmet moves up, moves down.

And the woman Kishimo—she knows no parents, no girlhood nor husband. Pursued from chaos, stricken by a venemous sting, saved by the Aizen—like us, she seeks some future the sight of which is obscured by mists.

Down, up. Okinu-nushi stands, cold droplets falling from helmet to cuirass to *kogake* to frozen earth.

You are the Spirit Master, Susano-wu wails. Yours is power! Summon up those shades who can give us counsel! If you yourself will give us none, summon those who will!

Silence, and the wail of the sea wind replaces the wail of the errant chamberlain. There is the silent mockery of the Spirit Master. But now Okinu-nushi raises his arm and draws a great circle overhead, darkness springing into being at the passage of his pointing finger. The sky above the grassy bluff where four figures stand grows dark. Crystalline blue is obscured by roiling darkness, a darkness more that of clouds than of night, more like mist than clouds, more like cold black smoke than mist.

The wind drops.

The air chills.

The sun, the Mirror of Amaterasu, shines as ever across the

choppy dark waters. It has risen now, well into the sky, and yet for all its impeded glare the light that it gives is lessened by a half; the warmth, by nine parts of ten.

Okinu-nushi drops his hand once more to his side and the darkness roiling overhead expands to the horizons of the world. Come then, the Spirit Master intones. Without awaiting response, he turns and strides toward the woods that border the grassy bluff. The three follow wordlessly.

The woods that had appeared green and lush and welcoming in the warm sunlight now appear dark and forbidding. Their greenery is no longer a bright and vivacious shade but a dark and forbidding one, darker than the green of pine needles. The leaves are not fleshy but dry and shriveled; the branches are skeletal, brittle in appearance. As the wind passes through the boughs and leaves it no longer sings and sighs but instead moans and shrieks.

Okinu-nushi the Spirit Master leads the way across the grassy plain to the forest. He passes beneath the reaching boughs of the nearest trees and Kishimo, as she steps beneath the canopy of horrid branches, slows her step one instant to peer back at the Mirror of Amaterasu, now a watery pale disk half obscured by racing sheets of smoky cloud. A gasp involuntarily escapes her cold lips and she turns back to follow the dark Master.

With each step of the Spirit Master there appears a circle of white frost about his *kogake,* foot armor. As he passes onward, the frost fades away, leaving whatever moss, fern, grassling, or leaves he has touched a withered gray-brown beside which even the depressed greenish-black of the forest floor appears lively.

A few piercing-eyed birds, perched dimly on gnarled and twisted tree limbs, peer silently at the passing quartet.

Water accumulated from past storms drops sullenly from black limbs, forming puddles of frozen black mush beneath the vegetable canopy.

With each passing stride the numbing cold increases. Dripping water forms rows of white ice stalactites from tree limbs; the icicles receive no direct sunlight and hence yield up no prismatic glints but instead seem to glow with a ghastly gray-white luminescence, partly refracted ambient light that manages to filter half heartedly through layers of branches and dispirited leaves, the remainder seemingly a dismal glow inherent in the water itself.

Someplace deep in the woods, far from the makeshift trail of the three following the Spirit Master, a water stalactite looses its grip on the wood of its spawning and falls to the cold black soil beneath. It strikes and buries its needle-sharp tip deep in the bosom of the earth with a moist sound like that of a *yanagi-ba,* willow-leaf spear tip, lodging itself deeply in the flesh of an ill-protected warrior.

Elsewhere a dead limb in some upper reach of the forest cracks beneath the doubled weight of an ice coating and rows of icy stalactites, and plunges, crashing and bounding, through layers and ranks of lower limbs, knocking loose fragile icicles, landing finally amidst the tinkle of thousands of shards of shattered crystal ice.

In a space where some score of heavy-boled cedars form a dark grove, the Spirit Master Okinu-nushi halts. He stands in the center of a circular clearing facing Kishimo, Aizen, Susano-wu. Okinu-nushi reaches beneath the armored skirt of his cuirass and pulls forth a *so-men,* full-face mask of sculpted metal that fits between the brim of his iron *kabuto* helmet and the edge of his *tanko*-style armored cuirass. The *so-men* hides the dim smoky mystification of the dark Master's face although his deep glowing eyes gleam all the more menacingly through the narrow eye-slits of the metal face.

Sit! the Spirit Master commands Kishimo, Aizen, Susano-wu, his deep and sepulchral voice echoing from the metal face's immobile, down-drawn mouth. Sit! rebounds from the dozen thick-boled cedars.

With a rustle the three obey, settling quickly to the cold, damp ground. Within the circle of the cedars there is no growth, no greenery: only black, damp soil.

Okinu-nushi the Spirit Master stands beneath an opening to the blackened, tormented sky, *kogake*-armored feet planted wide, *hoshi-kabuto* helmet thrown back, arms raised. Kishimo watches and waits. Okinu-nushi lowers head and arms. In the grayness of the clearing, the dark metal of his helmet and armor stands darkly against the nearly black backdrop of naked and splintery trees.

The dark Master, facing Kishimo and her companions, turns slowly in a circle, another, more rapidly, turning, turning, no lightness coming from him, only the deep glare of his masked eyes flashing from time to time. He revolves faster and faster, arms extended to draw a circle about his feet at the length of an iron-tipped arrow.

Streaks of somber lightning flash through the clouds overhead. The sound of rustles and cracking limbs creeps from the cedar-and-pine forest. The drip of cold water from limb to limb to moist chilled earth makes a steady patter.

From somewhere out of sight mixed odors emerge: the hot, harsh one of smoldering coals; the cold, brackish scent of seaweed and salt spray; the too-sweet odor of uncleaned wounds and unburied dead; the pungent cleansing darts of camphor and cedar.

Kishimo's legs tremble beneath her, or perhaps the earth itself trembles beneath her feet.

Okinu-nushi is a gray half cone now, the peak of his iron helmet the point of the half cone, the gray of his armor its spreading shaft, the damp earth beneath his feet its base. From the Spirit Master's spinning form there comes a weird music: Kishimo hears the moan of wind generated by the Master's own twirling speed as it roars and writhes through the plates and lacings of his armor; from the throat of the Master comes a low chanting of words meaningless to the Kishimo, the Aizen, the errant Susano-wu.

From deep within the forest there comes a wailing, a moaning, an answer to the chant of the Spirit Master. Kishimo turns to look in the direction of the sound, to her flank, beyond the unmoving figure of the man-god Aizen. A dim glow appears and a form emerges from between the ranked tree boles.

Tall and desiccated, garbed in long kimono and cloth court

cap, *naga-eboshi,* white-bearded and dead-white of face, a bard paces into the clearing, ignores Kishimo and Aizen and Susano-wu, bows to the Spirit Master, stands surrounded by faint light, silent.

From the opposite sides comes a wailing, a moaning, Kishimo turns. A figure emerges from between two cedars: beardless but as pale as the first, wearing court robes, headband, tattered *hakama* breeches. The newcomer bows also to Okinu-nushi; he, too, pays no heed to the three others facing the Spirit Master.

Slowly the Master's spinning slows. The moan and shriek of air drops lower in pitch until it is no longer audible. The features of armor, *kabuto,* leering *so-men* metal mask become visible once more. The glowing eyes of the Spirit Master gleam through the openings of the *so-men* mask.

The Spirit Master bows to the white-bearded bard.

Hieda no Are, the Spirit Master names the bard.

The Master turns, bows to the second, robed figure.

The dark Master inclines his head: O Yasumaro, he acknowledges the scholar.

The two pale shadows bow to the Spirit Master, then once again to each other. They appear unaware of the presence of the three travelers. Each shade carries an ancient scroll book and writing brush. Each speaks the name of the other:

O Yasumaro.

Hieda no Are.

The Spirit Master has summoned. We have come. We have come from the pleasures of Hell. We have come to the Forest of Ice in response to the summons of the Spirit Master. Speak your will, dark Master, that we may satisfy it and begone.

Okinu-nushi whispers to the shades who stand listening. The woman Kishimo, the man-god Aizen, the errant chamberlain of the land of Yomi, Susano-wu: all observe.

The two shades nod.

Hieda no Are, bowing, raises scroll, uses writing brush as a pointer, reads aloud a prophecy of the quest of the three. Hieda no Are, pale and elongated in *naga-eboshi* cap, long kimono, white beard, gives prophecy in a reedy, sing song voice. He reads from the Records of Ancient Matters, the *Kojiki*. His voice is thin and high but his words are clear: doom, failure, death. For the three, doom and failure and death. Long struggle, pain and bleeding, terror and travail, hopes dashed, no salvation.

Ichijitsu.

The Way of the One and Only Truth.

Doom, failure, death for Aizen-myu, Susano-wu, the Kishimo.

Hieda no Are bows, replaces his scroll beneath his kimono, writing brush tucked within his tattered *obi;* his words, directed to Okinu-nushi, heard no less by the three travelers. Now Hieda no Are falls silent.

O Yasumaro speaks.

Ichijitsu is denied; in its place O Yasumaro proposes the doctrine of Truth in Two Parts. Citing the Chronicles of the Land, *Nihonji,* O Yasumaro brings objections to the hopelessness of the prophecy of Hieda no Are. Doom, failure, death are denied. Long struggle, pain and bleeding, terror and travail, all of these O Yasumaro agrees will come.

But that hopes will be dashed, salvation denied, O Yasumaro refuses to predict.

Truth in Two Parts. The travelers to decide their own fate. Struggle and sacrifice to win their rewards.

The bearded Hieda no Are casts long fingers beneath his *obi,* withdraws his fine black lacquered writing brush with its thin, stiff bristles. He bows to Okinu-nushi the Spirit Master, holding writing brush before him in two hands. Spirit Master bows in return. Hieda no Are turns and bows to the scholar O Yasumaro.

O Yasumaro draws his own writing brush from *obi.* It is lacquered with a color that shimmers like gold. He bows to Hieda no Are, to Okinu-nushi, who returns his bow, to Hieda no Are once more.

Each draws scroll from kimono; the bard, *Kojiki;* the scholar, *Nihonji.* They present brush and scroll like samurai with sword and *te-date,* hand-held shield.

Both bow, rise, present.

Kishimo blinks as, in the gloom of the clearing in the Forest of Ice, the writing brush of each shade elongates to become a flashing, polished *tachi* longsword; the scroll of each, an oblong *te-date* shield of decorated metal.

The hilt of the *tachi* of Hieda no Are is worked with gleaming black enamel; that of O Yasumaro, with yellow gold.

The scholar strikes first. The blow of his sword is caught by the upper edge of O Yasumaro's shield.

O Yasumaro swings *tachi* overhead and downward. The blow is deflected by the sword of his opponent, glancing from ornate *tsuba,* sword-hilt guard.

Two opponents circle warily; three travelers watch in silence; Spirit Master stands in center of icy ring, turning slowly to keep glowing eyes fixed upon combatants.

Bard leaps, twirling *tachi* longsword overhead, brings blade in flashing sweep halfway between vertical and horizontal as if to cleave head from trunk.

Scholar twists to avoid blow. Wearing no armor, O Yasumaro's sword arm is severed at shoulder and skitters across frozen ground, still clutching *tachi* by decorative enamel hilt.

Hai! Hieda no Are advances, swinging *tachi* in flashing circles overhead, ready to finish his opponent.

O Yasumaro dances backward. No blood flows from his wound.

Hieda no Are swings *tachi* against his opponent but sword bounds from shield one time, two, again.

The severed sword arm of O Yasumaro rises to shoulder height, speeds through chill air to stand beside bard, facing against Hieda no Are.

Hieda no Are, appalled, slashes at the arm but to no avail. After failures he returns to attack O Yasumaro. Hieda no Are strikes at O Yasumaro. As he does so, the floating arm sweeps bright sword in a horizontal arc and the head of Hieda no Are, eyes popped wide in astonishment, white beard streaming, flies from its place and bounds to the feet of the Spirit Master.

The head rolls to an upright posture upon its jagged neck,

eyes flashing, observes the battle between O Yasumaro and Hieda no Are. The body of Hieda no Are is blind and its head, observing the battle, cries warnings and directions to the body.

Slash! Dodge! Advance! Turn!

The battle rages: arm against headless bard, sword against one-arm scholar.

Kishimo watches in cold satisfaction.

Beneath black-cloud gray sky there is no way to measure the progress of the day. Water continues to drip from leaf to limb, puddles freeze, and stalagmites of ice grow from the earth.

At length Okinu-nushi the Spirit Master grows impatient with the conduct of the ghosts. He claps his hands. Bard and scholar fade into nothingness.

The metal mask of Okinu-nushi seems to raise the corners of its lips in a ghastly smile.

Travelers, Okinu-nushi shouts with a voice that shakes stalactites from tree limbs so that they tinkle to the ground in heaps, what fun! What a show! I have had more pleasure from this than from any event in a thousand years!

Travelers, the eight-headed serpent awaits!

Travelers, I join your party!

Okinu-nushi roars with laughter.

II

No further word is spoken. Kishimo looks at her companions. The Aizen nods, Susano-wu grunts his affirmation. This is as close as conversation approaches.

The Spirit Master Okinu-nushi has delayed for no reply, nor was his statement made to evoke any response. A peasant may ask his rice to grow; a warrior, the skies to provide a snow covering for telltale tracks. But the dark Master makes no requests. The bard and the scholar he summoned and dismissed. He has told the travelers that he will join their party —perhaps, more in verity, that they will be attached to him as companions and retainers—and makes no pause for consideration or response.

The Spirit Master turns his back upon Kishimo and the others and moves off through the cedars and pines, through the chill-water-dripping Forest of Ice. The feet of Okinu-nushi seem hardly to touch the ground as he strides forward. Rather he glides as a sled drawn across a frozen pond, moving with graceful ease, a ring of frost springing into being with each stride, remaining behind as Okinu-nushi advances, fading slowly —Kishimo glances behind herself to be assured of this—after his passage.

Overhead, the limbs of half-frozen trees cross and twine like the arms of husband and wife crossing snow-covered millet field, embracing for warmth rather than love. Little winds spring up and fade away; between their hisses, their mysterious whispers of secrets unrevealed, the brushes and rustlings of needles and leaves, there come still the plashings of drops as they fall from trees to earth, shimmer briefly in the light, even the dim and diffuse daylight of the Forest of Ice.

Time is lost to Kishimo; the Mirror of Amaterasu is long since lost and in place of blue sky and golden sun there is only endless gray, gray-black limbs and leaves woven overhead and shimmering pearl-gray in the scarce breaks between the trees. There is no path to be seen, only the choice of the gliding Okinu-nushi. Yet the Forest of Ice is free of underbrush. There are only trees and earth, frozen ponds and puddles, white stalagmites writhing upward from the earth as if seeking to break free and speed away, graceful crystalline figures of birds and great insects, animals and human figures, each trapped within a prison of cold translucence, awaiting the touch, the word, the moment to spring away from the chill that holds them, that chains them to the black earth.

By imperceptible degrees the Forest of Ice grows darker. Trees, gray-black, grow blacker. Patches of visible sky, pearl-gray, grow darker and darker until, passing beneath a small circular opening in the leaf roof of the forest, Kishimo pauses momentarily to gaze upward and observes a black roof over the universe, a roof sprinkled with the icy glitter of white, blue, green points of light.

The stars.

She continues ahead. The party has become strung out: Okinu-nushi leads, gliding steadily between cedars and pines, setting a pace not difficult for Kishimo to match but one pauseless, ceaseless, merciless. She follows him. He never glances back. Behind comes Aizen-myu, the Aizen, the man-god, dogging the steps of Kishimo. Behind the Aizen, the errant chamberlain of the court of the Dragon King comes: Susano-wu. Kishimo glances behind from time to time, sees the others following.

There is little light in the Forest of Ice, yet sufficient for guiding the feet of a careful traveler. The hard brilliance of starlight, the gentler radiance of the moon—even where the leafy canopy blocks Kishimo's sight of the sky, the streaming light is scattered and mirrored by brilliant ice sheaths that coat many limbs and by stalagmites rising beneath the trees. Other mounds lying under the cedars and pines reflect even more brilliantly, turning the faint white light of the distant sky-lanterns into shattered spectra of red, purple, blue, green-yellow.

Here and there an ice-coated mound glows from within: some creature furnished by the gods with a luminous organ, trapped and frozen in an all but invisible jacket of ice, glaring still, glimmering like a ghost of itself.

And from farther into the woods, other lights, moving ghostly lights, flicker and refract off the ice-covered trunks of trees like the hand-carried lamps of unseen persons: pilgrims? bandits? warriors? Kishimo recovers herself with a shudder and hastens to remain close behind Okinu-nushi. The Spirit Master is himself visible by a faint luminosity. His decorated *hoshi-kabuto,* his old-style armor, his weapons, his skin itself emit a pale glow that gives him the appearance of a specter gliding silently ahead of the three others. The occasional scrape or rattle of his iron equipment adds to the weirdness of the time even more than would absolute silence. At last the cedars and pines grow fewer; the canopy of limbs and leaves and needles above opens. The trees stand more sparsely, giving way to a region of bushes and grass. The open sky holds more stars than there were fish in the Sea of Mists. The great light of the moon rivals the sun, the Mirror of Amaterasu, in brilliance. The grass slopes downward and ends at a broad band of what appears as recently fallen snow, wind-rippled and pallid beneath the brilliant moon, stretching away at either hand and curving, then, into the distance.

The moon has passed its zenith and in its slow tumble to the earth's horizon its rays cast long shadows of blue from the cold white snow-ripples.

Okinu-nushi strides across white crystals, his armored feet making a soft sliding sound with each step, leaving behind him only the faintest suggestion of a trail as his graceful gliding gait carries him nearly clear of the surface underfoot.

Kishimo follows the Spirit Master. With her first stride into the region beyond the grassy slope she is startled to discover that the rippled dunes are not of snow at all, but of cold white sand. The band of shadowy ripples gives upon a black flatness, and even as Kishimo stands observing, a fresh cold wind springs up, sweeping across the roof of the Forest of Ice, growing colder as it does so, then swooping away, down the grassy plain and the rippled sands; beyond the sand the wind sets up sparkling rows of wavelets on the surface of the black lake.

Beyond the lake, Kishimo's eyes follow reflected shards of moonlight; the vista is too distant and dim to perceive clearly, but the star-sprinkled heaven is blotted out in a skyline sharply marked by more trees. The Spirit Master has led them not to the end of the Forest of Ice but merely to a larger clearing where a black lake of chilly depths laps and glimmers in the moonlight.

At the edge of the water the Spirit Master halts and gestures, chanting a summons. The water bubbles and seethes. Four great heads burst through the surface and rear high above the tall Spirit Master, still farther above Kishimo, Aizen, Susano-wu. In an instant Kishimo recognizes four great beasts, four beasts of the sort that carried her along with the Aizen-myu from the lush land of her earlier awakening to the ship *Ofuna* in the Sea of Mists, and later from the nameless raider craft to the Land of Gloom, Yomi.

The mind of the beast has been a puzzle. On both journeys it has obeyed the command of Aizen, but so a bullock obeys the command of the rice farmer, an armored horse obeys the command of the samurai, the house dog obeys the command of its master. The awareness and the understanding of such creatures is imponderable, their obedience as likely blind submission to command as knowing act of comradeship with master and friend.

As for these great creatures with their bulging segmented bodies, faceted eyes, membranous wings, numerous trailing legs —Kishimo now obtains her best vision of them as they rise from the black waters into the silver-and-gold-rippling moonlight and advance, dripping and glistening in the night, to the snow-toned sand.

Their form, Kishimo realizes, is like that of titanic wasps, and the similarity is emphasized by their conduct, for, ignoring the oddly variegated quartet of Spirit Master, man-god, errant chamberlain-samurai, and dark-haired woman, the great creatures perform a ceremony of their own, buzzing and dancing, raising leg or wing or unsheathed stinger, circling, droning, darting forward or back, rising with whir of wings the distance of a spear-cast above the rippled sand, then dropping once more, creeping about in circles or oblongs or spirals or loops, raising and dropping the pitch and volume of their buzzing, touching one another, leaping back and finally arriving at some agreed posture, arraying themselves as if to pursue the four winds, the quartet of travelers left standing clustered at the center of the great insects' figure.

Without speaking, Okinu-nushi advances to the side of the beast nearest himself and rises to mount it. Aizen, Susano-wu, do likewise with their own beasts. Kishimo, too, settling herself alone at the familiar perch previously shared with the Aizen.

The beasts rise unprompted, beating the cold night air with delicate wings of shimmering translucence. As they rise above the black lake at the center of the Forest of Ice, Kishimo wonders whether the creature bearing her is the same that carried her earlier with the Aizen, but she has no way of knowing. There is no sound here save the drone of the four beasts' pairs of wings and the rush of night past the faces of the four travelers. Kishimo casts her eyes upward at the bright roundness of the moon and wonders if the beasts are carrying herself and her companions thither, there to meet whatever wonders or horrors may lie in wait. But after rising, rising, they settle into a steady pace that quickly leaves behind the black forest, the white ring of sand, the jet-colored waters broken by bands and flickers of reflected light.

The beating of the great wasps' wings steadies into a lulling, rhythmic drone. The three companion beasts and their riders are easily visible, Aizen and Susano-wu in the strong moonlight, bright rays reflecting off the dragon helms of their *hoshi-kabutos* and their lacquered accouterments, the Spirit Master Okinu-nushi, brighter than the others in the steady glow of his own luminosity, his back turned to Kishimo as his beast sets the pace and the path of the party, his metal mask and deep glowing eyes turned away and hidden from Kishimo's sight.

The million stars burn and twinkle.

A sense of timelessness and tranquility descends upon Kishimo. The puzzles of her origin and ultimate destiny, twin reflecting glasses defining the limitations of her awareness, cease to be of major importance to her and she finds herself floating in stability, the earth, ice fields, island and lakes, the isle of the Forest of Ice, the Sea of Mists, the Land of Gloom, drifting beneath and behind; overhead, drifting wisps of cloud, black sky dotted with glittering gem-stars and the moon huge and brilliant, its features clear and almost painfully visible; behind her, Aizen and Susano-wu astride their giant mounts; ahead, Okinu-nushi. Even the horizon is visible, although far distant, curving like the skin of a giant apple.

Despite the rush of wind whipping Kishimo's hair and whistling in her ears, the world has settled to a state of contentment. The wings of her wasp-beast drone steadily, its body and her own throbbing to the rhythm of their sweep. Kishimo's head nods in a state close to sleep but not identical to it. She is still, vaguely and distantly and warmly, aware of her surroundings. One hand rests on the lacquered hilt of her sword, the other lies unmoving in her lap.

Somehow she becomes attuned to a set of thoughts, neither human nor god-like, not her own nor those of any of her three companions.

She senses an eagerness, a great and joyous anticipation. The four beasts share a single mind, a conjoint consciousness, and all—or all, as one—beat through the high air in search of a single reward. Kishimo cannot decide what it is—something sweet, something precious, something that the wasps desire above any other material good. It is like honey yet not the same, it is like nectar yet not the same.

But Kishimo knows that the eight-headed serpent possesses the substance that is of little interest to human or to god but is most precious to the wasps. And the beasts know that the serpent dwells in the western land of Izumo at the mouth of the river Hi. And Kishimo knows that the four great beasts are bearing their riders to the land of Izumo to find the creature, the serpent, where the serpent must be conquered before Susano-wu can ever obtain the sword Kuzanagi or the four great wasps the precious nectar that they desire.

The Mirror of Amaterasu rises once more over the eastern sea, turning the clouds above Kishimo to bursts of crimson and golden splendor with its early rays, sending the stars to hide and the moon to fade, turning the jet-black night-heaven to the clear blue day-heaven. No birds soar so high as the giant wasps, no sparrow of field, no tern of strand nor albatross of sea. Only the four great insects and their four armed riders, and where the sea glitters and leaps in the east, the sun, the Mirror of Amaterasu, blazes hot and white.

Before very long the warmth of the morning sun replaces the chill of night air. Kishimo feels herself growing warm. The sun fills the world with its brightness.

Ahead of the wasps and beneath them to one side Kishimo sees the black etching of land upon the silver-blue mirror of sea. The wasps surge forward as if they can scent from here the nectar of their wishes. The land grows larger and its jagged black gives way to suggestions of green. The wasps drop lower in the morning sky, the air growing warmer as they drone onward, closer to the face of the water. The ice and storms of the Sea of Mists, the terrible chill of the Forest of Ice, fade away even from memory and the air itself becomes warm, moist, like a thousand hands caressing the cheeks and the body of Kishimo, like a warm perfume caressing her nostrils and her lungs.

The land ahead is Izumo, and glistening where the land meets the warm western sea is the mouth of the river Hi, broad and sluggish and silvery.

The wasps drop lower and lower. The land appears beneath

their many folded legs, their gleaming faceted eyes, the land warm and prosperous in appearance, with fields of millet and of rice, many wooden boats fitted with sails or oars or stream-sweeps anchored on the river Hi or moving leisurely up and down its gently flowing surface, peasant shacks and prosperous farmers' and traders' houses built over the edges of the river on wooden stilts or sitting in the midst of growing fields of food grains.

This is the land of Izumo, but there rests upon it a dark shadow, one cast neither by floating cloud nor by flying beast. It is the shadow of the serpent.

The wasps drop to earth near a little cluster of farmers' huts built at the edge of a river village. From the back of her mount Kishimo sees the farmers and boatmen moving slowly about. The sun is warm, the morning air pleasantly scented with the odor of clean flowing river water and rich growing crops, yet there is a heaviness, a lethargy, in the figures of the people as they move.

Kishimo drops from the back of her wasp and sees Okinu-nushi and Aizen and Susano-wu do the same. The beasts rise and confer in the heavy air, then, agreed, plunge beneath the surface of the river Hi for reasons not known to Kishimo. Susano-wu approaches Kishimo; the man-god Aizen-myu and the Spirit Master Okinu-nushi walk together to investigate the condition of the river Hi.

In all the village, the most somber house is one with darkened windows and shrouded door. Kishimo and Susano-wu beg entry and, invited, enter the house.

An elderly farmer and wife sit within, rocking and grieving. Kishimo asks the cause of their grief and of the somber mood of all the countryside.

It is the time of the sacrifice to the serpent, the farmer explains to her. The village and the fields and the river must yield up their most beautiful children to the serpent for its meal, or the serpent, raging, will destroy all the countryside and kill farmer and fisher-folk alike.

And the farmer and his wife, old people both, barren for all their lives, have been blessed with the birth of a beautiful child, a chubby girl-child with glossy hair and great shining eyes who smiles for her parents and holds out her arms to be lifted and cuddled.

The village and the fields and the river must yield up their most beautiful children, Susano-wu repeats. Then he asks the farmer and his wife: How many children? And to what fate are they sent?

The farmer, rocking sadly, says this: Eight children, four boys and four girls. The dragon-serpent possesses eight necks, eight mouths, and appears once in eight years to demand eight tender morsels.

Why do the people not flee?

This they tried once, long ago. The dragon-serpent pursued them. The serpent possesses an unconquerable sword, which it used to cut down forest and fortress alike until it caught the people and in its rage slew eight-times-eight children. So the people now live in fear and misery. They postpone weddings and try to bear children at the beginning of each eight years, so that they may grow tall and hard by the end of seven years. In the eighth year the people send them away to save them.

But always the heavens send some in other years. And the cruel trick of the heavens has been to send to the farmer and his wife their darling at the time of the eighth year. Not yet walking, plump and jolly, their darling will be a perfect morsel for the serpent's meal. She and seven other children gathered from village, field, and river.

The farmer's wife wails and strikes her husband. Dirty lecher! she terms him. Lustful wretch! Oh, that I yielded to you! Oh, had I but resisted, we would have no daughter to give up to the serpent! I never knew when I was well off, husband! I mourned my barrenness and now I mourn my fruitfulness!

Show me the child, Susano-wu commands.

The farmer says, Yes, Lord Samurai, and instructs his wife to bring the girl. The farmer's wife brings her forth dressed in miniature kimono and *obi,* her hair brushed and tied with a red ribbon. She shows the baby to Susano-wu and to Kishimo.

Kishimo's woman's heart is pained to think of the death of the girl. She reaches and the woman places the baby in her arms. Kishimo holds the plump bundle close to her, cuddling the soft cheek to her warm bosom. The infant looks at Kishimo with great dark eyes; with chubby fingers she explores the long hair hanging on Kishimo's breast. Kishimo draws in breath sharply and hands the baby back to her mother.

Susano-wu strikes one fist upon the palm of his other hand. Old people! he says, his voice harsh with anger and remorse. Old people! The sword of the demon dragon-serpent is the sword Kuzanagi! It is the heirloom of my family, lost many generations ago to this demon! I pledge upon the tarnished honor of my family that the serpent shall die, the sword shall be recovered, and your girl-child shall not be sacrificed, nor any other, ever again, to the monster!

The shame upon my family, Susano-wu continues, the shame rests upon me, and even *hara-kiri* could not atone for it, for the shame would continue to grow with each eighth year forever. Only the destruction of the serpent and the recovery of the sword Kuzanagi can begin to make up for lost honor!

I will face the dragon-serpent and restore what honor I can!

Susano-wu strides from the old farm couple's hut, leaving farmer and farmer's wife standing together, arms about each other like youthful lovers, their fat daughter held closely between them, cooing and chortling, unaware of the drama of the day.

Kishimo follows Susano-wu from the hut. Side by side they walk to a long wooden pier that runs from the village street to the center of the river Hi. Here they see the man-god Aizen-myu standing before the dark Master Okinu-nushi.

You have learned of what will happen? Kishimo asks the others.

The Spirit Master remains silent but Aizen says, Yes, we have learned of the sacrifice demanded and the penalty for its refusal. What plans have you made?

Kishimo does not answer; rather, Susano-wu speaks: I will confront the serpent. I will destroy the demon and recover the sword Kuzanagi. Thus will I retrieve the honor of my family.

What assistance may we give? asks Aizen.

None, replies the errant Susano-wu. Then: No, I err. Kishimo may aid me now in one act, and you, Aizen-myu, later.

The two, as one, ask: In what way, Susano-wu?

The errant chamberlain points to Kishimo. The monster dwells in a cavern beneath the river Hi, Susano-wu asserts. Draw back the waters that I may face him in clear air and on dry earth.

Kishimo draws the jewel of the ebbing tide, the Kanjiu jewel, from its place within her *obi*. She holds it to her brow and commands the river Hi to draw back, and as the four stand upon the end of the long pier a circular current swirls beneath their gaze. A space of open sand half as wide as the river becomes clear at its center, and at the center of this, a dark opening from which a slither and a hiss rise to be heard by all.

Susano-wu leaps from the pier and lands upright on the dry sand before the pitch-black pit.

12

Susano-wu advances carefully; Kishimo, standing on the pier with Okinu-nushi the Spirit Master and Aizen-myu the man-god, watches closely, her breath drawn in tension. Villagers and farmers line the shore of the river Hi. Boatmen hold their wooden craft in place with long poles or cast anchors, safely away from the brink of water thrown up by the power of the Kanjiu jewel.

The errant chamberlain, armor bright beneath the Mirror of Amaterasu, advances carefully across the gleaming, freshly exposed sand. Fish flop and struggle, gleaming silver and white as the sunlight rebounds from their scales; Susano-wu kindly circles the new sandy plain created by the Kanjiu jewel, lifting each fish in his arms and carrying it to the wall of water that surrounds the sandy clearing. He presses each finny creature into the water wall, and Kishimo, watching, sees silvery creatures, each in its turn, circle and bow in gratitude before taking departure for the farther regions of the river Hi.

Crabs pop from beneath the sand and scuttle away from the feet of Susano-wu. Not requiring assistance, they speed across the sand, warrior faces on their shells frowning angrily at the unwelcome light and heat of the Mirror. Sea shrubs and trees lie flaccid, unable to stand without the aid of the waters of the Hi, awaiting the return of the waters before resuming their graceful postures.

Susano-wu approaches the brink of the pit. Kishimo, straining, still can see nothing but blackness there. The sounds from the pit are as strong as ever: a slithering and scraping as of some terrible moist creature moving with instinctive but needless stealth to creep upon some victim, more prey than rival.

Beside the pit Susano-wu cries out.

The slithering ceases for a moment, then resumes more loudly than before—and dark tentacles of a shade of green barely distinguishable from black appear above the rim of the pit, waving and swaying, sparkling in their wetness with the reflected light of the Mirror. Other objects, frilled and lacy, with great dark gleaming circles of eyes and huge, red, fanged maws, waver and jerk among the tentacles.

Susano-wu bows before the monster.

From one of the horrid mouths a small cloud erupts, black and roiling with faults and streaks of dark crimson. To Kishimo there is a strange familiarity to the sight, yet even as she watches, the cloudlets ripple and float skyward, dissipating in the clear air before they reach the level of the tops of the green swaying trees that line the banks of the Hi.

Susano-wu seats himself carefully on the sand near the edge of the pit. He calls loudly to the creature, so loudly that his voice echoes across the sandy plain, off the watery walls that quiver and bend with each moment. Each word, though bent and altered by the echoes, is still clear to the ears of Kishimo.

Lord Serpent, Susano-wu cries, Lord Serpent, attend the chamberlain of Ryujin the Dragon King of the Sea, emissary of Yomi, Land of Gloom.

The serpent stretches several heads high above the brink of the pit and hisses its reply to Susano-wu. Each word is spoken by a different head in turn, the fringes and plates and horns of the heads quivering and glistening in the sunlight, the mouths giving out ugly puffs of smoke with each word, every cloudlet black and dense yet each lined with streaks of color, each color as different as the head from which it issues.

Black with red, black with yellow, black with brilliant gleaming blue, with green, orange, ugly purple, metallic gold, and from the greatest and most fearsome head of all, a cloud of blackness marked with a deeper blackness that speaks not of night and peace but of death and mourning.

You, chamberlain, the serpent hisses. You lackey. What is your wish?

Sitting, Susano-wu inclines head and trunk politely. But return what is my family's, and promise to leave the people of the river Hi to live without sacrificing their children, Serpent, and I and my companions will depart in peace.

The serpent roars, a terrible sound made one part of angry shout, one part of laughing derision, one part of louder hissing. Return that which is your family's, chamberlain? What have I that is your family's? Why suggest that I would stain my being with the belongings of slaves?

Susano-wu, ignoring the insult, replies: The sword Kuzanagi, which you took from an ancestor, thus bringing shame upon my house for all generations thence to this, Lord Serpent. I will have back the sword Kuzanagi from your toils.

Again the serpent roars, this time more angrily and with less of good nature than of the evil intent earlier displayed. Puny being, you provide no amusement. Go away, go away, let back the waters of the river Hi and begone—else be destroyed.

Ah, ah, Susano-wu nods. Do not dismiss me so quickly, Lord Serpent. You will not destroy me so easily, so best to listen to my words and grant my petition.

The serpent rears high above the edge of the pit, all its heads roaring at once. One neck darts forward and its fangs snap at the seated chamberlain. But Susano-wu, a short distance away, manages a polite waist bow even though seated. The head, black eyes glittering angrily and flashing green, draws back.

Brother, another head hisses, its black eyes flashing yellow, brother, do not act so precipitously. Now, speck, this head says, addressing itself to Susano-wu, that was a clever trick of yours, dodging away from my brother.

Susano-wu inclines his head. You are kind, Lord Serpent, he says. Be more kind yet and return to me the sword Kuzanagi, and free the people of the river Hi and this land of their sacrifices, and gladly will I leave you in peace and take my companions with me.

A head wreathed in shaggy, scaly frills leans forward, its great dark eyes flashing purple so palely as to approach the tint of roses. Worm, this head hisses, black smoke flashing purply-pink rising from its nostrils; worm, your trick provided us with a moment's mild diversion. Take your life now and escape or die.

Ah, ah, Susano-wu replies, that cannot be. But perhaps you will consent to negotiate, Lord Serpent. A small sip before we enter our serious discussion.

The chamberlain reaches within his kimono and brings forth a graceful, decorated procelain jug and nine tiny cups. These he sets carefully on the sand before himself. He gathers a few scraps of driftwood, all from within the reach of his arms, and piles them before him. He speaks to the little pile of wood, words not clear to the ears of Kishimo, still standing, watching and listening with the Spirit Master and the Aizen-myu, but at the end of Susano-wu's speech the driftwood bursts into bright little flames and heats the porcelain jug that the chamberlain places within the flames.

Susano-wu pours nine cups of steaming *sake* and raises one to the level of his eyes. Glancing across its rim, he says to the monster: Lord Serpent, honor this humble one by joining him.

Squirming across the bright sand from the black pit come eight green-black lengths, each tipped with a terrible head, frill-necked, ragged, hideous, round nostrils puffing black smoke, great eyes shining black and red, black and yellow, all the rest, and the chief head with mighty fangs and forked, flicking tongue, eyes black and black.

The eight terrible heads sniff at the eight tiny cups of steaming rice liquor while Susano-wu, nodding politely, sips at his own. The eight cups are emptied and the heads withdraw to the edge of the pit. Most of them drop beneath its edge. A few remain like the fingers of a mountain climber clutching the edge of a platform, glaring across the sand at Susano-wu, cloudlets of color-flashed black puffing from great round nostrils.

Surely the fish of the river Hi can provide nourishment for Lord Serpent, Susano-wu says softly. Leave aside the matter of the sword Kuzanagi for the moment, Lord Serpent. We shall return to the subject. But surely the beasts of the forests of the land of Izumo offer red meat and strength for Lord Serpent. The honor of my house has been taken, and I must strive for its recovery, but that is a subject to which we may revert at another time. Still, it is certain that the farmers of Izumo and the fisherman of the river Hi would gladly pay tribute to you in the form of bullocks and great nets full of fish if you would but spare their darling children. Why must you visit such loss upon these people, Lord Serpent?

Two or three heads slither about the sand like mighty snakes seeking their mates. This chamberlain might make a tasty morsel himself, black-and-orange eyes flashing, a fringed demon-head hisses. This bug must needs have his shell split down the back and the tender meat inside removed with care, black-eyes-blue-flashed hisses in return. This scaly grub should be dressed and roasted over his own charcoal, hisses black-eyes-flashed-gold.

Three terrible heads rise on ends of swaying, wavering rods and dart at Susano-wu, from left, from right, from before.

The errant chamberlain, calmly seated on warm sparkling sand a few paces away, carefully raises porcelain jug and refills eight tiny cups with steaming hot *sake*. Lord Serpent, he invites courteously, let us sip a bit of rice liquor and discuss our disagreements. Perhaps differences may be resolved without the spilling of blood.

Black-eyes-red-flashed, lying on edge of pit, turns to black-eyes-flashed-green. Clever, clever, black-eyes-red-flashed hisses. Did you see how he did that trick? Black-eyes-flashed-green responds: No, brother, but it was indeed a clever trick. Let us watch more closely. A clever, clever trick.

Susano-wu raises his *sake* cup, still partially filled, inclines his head, says: Please honor me, Lord Serpent.

Eight heads slither and weave across warm sand. At the edge

of the black pit a few tentacles slide over the sandy cusp, onto the flat before Susano-wu. Eight heads lap at hot *sake* with forked tongues. Ah, hisses black-eyes-black-flashed, not hot enough, not nearly hot enough.

Susano-wu bows his head. I crave pardon humbly. He places the *sake* jug in the hottest part of his little fire, adds more drift-twigs to make the flames higher and hotter. Shortly he retrieves the jug and fills eight cups once more. Eight heads lap at *sake*. Ah, several hiss, ah, better now, vile bug.

Susano-wu bows head in humble gratitude.

Four necks rise and wriggle, snake-like. Four great jaws open, four sets of gleaming fangs snap shut as necks vault forward from left, right, front, and rear of Susano-wu. The chamberlain gives no evidence of noticing the movement, but, a few bow-lengths away, gathers empty *sake* cups and places them in a circle about the little fire of driftwood and charcoal before him. Now the cups themselves as well as the *sake* jug are exposed to the heat of the flames.

Humbly, Susano-wu speaks. Perhaps, Lord Serpent, it was my manner of suggesting a change of diet that has proven offensive and that has prevented you, in your kind forebearance, from replying to my proposal.

Great eyes gleaming black flashed with gold, purple, orange, green, blink in astonishment. From the serpent's throats come hisses of amazement.

I fear that this diet of Hi children may prove unwholesome for the noble stomach—there is but one noble stomach?—of my Lord. Rather than scold so offensively as I did, I should better have suggested that more variety of morsels would provide greater pleasure and titillation to the eight palates of Lord Serpent, and greater stimulation to the noble stomach. All would thus lead to long life and great delectation, while this diet of eight babies each eight years must be a bore to one of such refined sensitivities as my Lord Serpent.

Reaching for the *sake* jug, Susano-wu fills the eight cups, all of them by now so hot that they have begun to glow red in the bright morning air. His own cup Susano-wu holds in one hand, adding from the *sake* jug a mere trickle to the liquor still remaining.

From the pit of the monster more tentacles creep, black-green and slimy, over the dug-out edge and onto the warming sand. All eight heads rest on the sand, and seem to roll their eyes at one another while tentacles wreath among them, creeping through scaly ruffs and over blinking, rolling eyes.

The great master head of the serpent, its eyes black flashed with black, its great jaw and snapping fangs larger and fiercer than those of any of the other seven, rises from the sand and wavers, confronting Susano-wu face to face. The horrid mouth opens and a puff of black roiling smoke emerges and drifts away skyward.

On the pier that extends over half the river Hi and half the newly exposed sand bank where Susano-wu sits, there is a stir. The woman Kishimo, standing at the end of the pier along with the Spirit Master Okinu-nushi and the man-god Aizen-myu, looks about and sees scores of timid villagers who have crept slowly onto the pier and edged along its length to see the strange confrontation in the dry center of the river. Here in the crowd Kishimo sees this one and that, apprehensively huddling over a small figure in kimono and *obi,* a boy- or girl-child slated for sacrifice to the serpent should Susano-wu fail in his trial.

Kishimo turns to Okinu-nushi. This being whom she confronts, this supernatural operator first encountered in the realm above Yomi, who performed his wondrous deeds in the Forest of Ice, Kishimo has not addressed before. Still, she says to him: Spirit Master! Spirit Master!

Okinu-nushi turns toward her, a cold wind and gray aura seeming to shift with his every graceful, gliding motion. The Spirit Master does not speak, but these glowing eyes set deep behind the fine-worked mask that he wears cast rays of frozen flame.

Kishimo shivers but she speaks. Spirit Master, Okinu-nushi, noble chamberlain Susano-wu faces the monster alone. Can you not assist? Summon up the spirits of the ancestors of Susano-wu who have shared the shames he expiates today. Let them aid him!

The corners of the metal mouth rise in a mirthless grin. Woman, the voice of Okinu-nushi echoes as if from a great remoteness, sounding like the faint cry of a distant pilgrim struggling through cold fog: Woman, ask no aid to be given the chamberlain. He will win over his foe or he will lose his own life and return to Yomi as the lowest of marine peasants, but he must find his own way in either case.

Kishimo makes no reply, but Okinu-nushi adds: As must we all. As must we all: deity, demigod, or mortal.

The Spirit Master turns away once more, the cold wind and dark aura sweeping over Kishimo as he moves, and once again Okinu-nushi and Kishimo, along with Aizen and the Hi people, give their attention to the business of Susano-wu and the demon-beast.

The errant chamberlain, face to face with the great black-eyed dragon-head, raises the hot *sake* jug in one hand, the monster's cup in the other, and pours. He lowers the *sake* jug to the fire, still holding filled cup before his face, and with his free hand reaches to draw his gleaming *tanto* shortsword from its scabbard, passed through the *obi* of his costume.

The Mirror of Amaterasu glints from the blade of Susano-wu's *tanto;* to Kishimo's eyes the bright image carries a momentary vision even of the *horimono,* the tutorial etchings on the blade of the sword. The *tanto* is dedicated, appropriately, to Amaterasu, whose symbol and friend is the sun, the Mirror.

The brilliance of the sun reflects from the blade. A glare passes over the master-head of the serpent. Kishimo can see the great black eyes gleaming.

Susano-wu holds *sake* cup in one hand, glittering *tanto* in the other, both before the dazzled eyes of the serpent. The serpent is speaking in a soft, hissing voice that slurs in Kishimo's ears into a drone, a buzz.

No meat so soft, no blood so sweet, the serpent hisses.

Sip the rice liquor, Lord, Susano-wu replies.

The tentacles writhe and tumble upon the sand like separate beasts at their gambol.

Sharp fangs in soft bellies, the serpent hisses. Fool bug, you who have never felt that flesh between your teeth cannot understand. There is no treat like Izumo baby. Ah, hum, hai!

Sip, Susano-wu coaxes. He waves the glittering *tanto* before the master-face of the serpent. The other heads, creeping on the stalks of their necks like snakes, have drawn closer to the two: black-eyes-flashed-yellow, black-eyes-red-flashed.

The drift-twig-and-charcoal fire, the *sake* jug, the cups, the chamberlain Susano-wu, all have placed themselves farther from the edge of the pit, near to the wall of cast-back Hi water where fish dart then halt, staring with flat broad eyes at the strange sight.

Susano-wu raises the cup for the master-head. The forked tongue darts out and the cup is emptied. Susano-wu reaches for the *sake* jug and fills the master-head's cup and those of the other seven, all of them drawn close to the little blaze on the sand. Heads and tentacles jostle to reach the cups. From the edge of the pit there is a horrid sucking sound and the body of the serpent-beast, a terrible glossy sack that wriggles and tumbles as if filled with life of its own, tumbles onto the sand.

Drink up, Susano-wu coaxes. He turns the blade of his *tanto* so that the reflected image of Amaterasu passes over sixteen terrible eyes, black flashed with blue, black flashed with gold. Eight heads dip. Eight forked tongues sip at glittering *sake,* steam rising to fill scaly nostrils.

The great serpent-head rises, its eyes glaring blearily at Susano-wu. Tender, tender meat, the serpent hisses.

Lord Serpent.

Tender meat, *ai!* And sweet blood. Hot, fresh blood.

Lord Serpent. Susano-wu bows.

Mite, fool, you will never regain the sword Kuzanagi, never regain your lost honor.

Lord Serpent. Susano-wu turns the *tanto, horimono* of the goddess Amaterasu flashing her Mirror the sun in the eyes of the great serpent-head, in the eyes of the lesser serpent-heads.

The terrible belly of the demon-beast writhes and jabs.

Seven heads fall to the warm sand, eyes aglaze: black-red, black-yellow, black-blue, black-green, black-orange, black-purple, black-gold.

The final head, the master-head of the monster, dragon-ruff flared, lunges, nostrils heaving, terrible fangs a-clash.

Susano-wu, a spear-length away, bows humbly. He stands facing the monster, bows humbly. Lord Serpent. Susano-wu kneels, tips the roasting *sake* jug so that its contents fill his two cupped hands, upholds them to offer to the demon-beast.

Lord Serpent, he whispers.

Within the water wall nearby, four great shapes like giant wasps dart and flitter, greated faceted eyes gleaming.

The master serpent-head darts out a forked red tongue, laps each drop of hot *sake* from the hands of Susano-wu. Tender flesh, sweet sweet blood, the monster hisses, drops, the head lolling, the eyes aglaze, glaring at the *tanto* of Susano-wu, at the *horimono* of the sun goddess, at the Mirror of Amaterasu.

It is hot on the sandy bottom of the river Hi. Steam rises from the drying river bed. Within the waters of the river Hi, hundreds of fish dart and gaze, four huge wasps stare with faceted eyes.

Susano-wu turns his back on the eight-headed serpent and strides to stand before the pier where Kishimo, Aizen-myu, Okinu-nushi watch and wait with the people of the river Hi, villagers, farmers, fishers. The chamberlain bows low, turns back, and strides to stand before the monster.

The chamberlain draws his *tachi,* longsword, bows to the Mirror of the sun goddess, then to the serpent. He stands above the first head, that with gold-flashed eyes. He lifts his sword, swings, *Hai!* the long blade flashes sunlight and cleanly severs the serpent-head.

Two other necks stir, eyes open blearily, a voice hisses: Did you feel—? Another responds: As in a dream, I thought—But both heads flop back onto sand, eyes closed.

Susano-wu strides to the next horrid neck, stands over black-eyes-flashed-purple. He lifts sword, swings, *hai!* again a head is severed. Again others shift restlessly, moan in disturbed dreams, become still once more. Again and again until only the master-head remains. Susano-wu bows, speaks: Lord Serpent, bug does thee honor. Susano-wu raises his sword, gazes briefly into the Mirror, swings downward with both hands locked tightly about the lacquered hilt of his *tachi*.

In the instant of frozen time, as the polished blade flashes in sunlight, slicing air on its way to slice neck, the glazed eyes glitter for a moment, the cold lips move as if to form a word.

Sweet.

Descending blade arrives, head rolls. Eight necks and many tentacles heave in a single violent convulsion. Susano-wu strides across steaming sand to the dancing belly of the serpent and with his shortsword slices a lengthy rent in the black disgusting leather. There is a great cry from within, as of many voices, and a hundred children tumble out, crying and cringing from the unaccustomed sunlight.

There is a louder answering cry from the river pier and villagers pour onto the sand, run to meet the rescued children, calling out: This is my child; This is my lad lost eight years to me; This is my girl lost sixteen years to me.

Old men and women worn by years of grief hobble on canes or crutches, gazing in wonder at children lost to them for forty years, for forty-eight years, infants fit to be the great-grandchildren of graybeard and his old woman, ancient parents peering through weak eyes at plump toddlers given to the awful serpent eight-times-eight years ago.

And there are children unclaimed, infants so long in the monster's belly that no parents survive to say they are theirs. Yet other villagers take these up, covering round cheeks and blinking, light-startled eyes with kisses and embraces. Old childless couples like the father and mother of Momotaro the little peachling-boy, or the aged bamboo cutter and his wife who once took in the tiny moon-goddess, take up orphan children and carry them joyfully in figures as the whole village makes a festival parade on the sandy floor of the river Hi.

A terrible splashing comes from the walled waters of the river, and four great wasp-creatures beat their way through the wall of water, across the drying sand, and to the carcass of the eight-necked serpent. Villagers grow pale, cry out in terror, but the wasps ignore the running people and head only for the lair of the beaten demon, the pit beneath the center of the river.

Quickly the four wasps, buzzing and humming their strange messages to one another, bustle into the pit. There emerges the sound of the four beasts gorging themselves on the nectar hoard of the serpent. Susano-wu strides boldly to the edge of the pit, braces arms and legs, and leaps audaciously into the center of the darkness. In a little while he re-emerges, clambering nimbly over the brink and onto the sand.

In his hand there flashes a light rivaling even that of the sun itself, a shimmering brilliance that runs up and down a shaft, blinding to the eye of any who gaze directly at it. Even with the eyes diverted, the bright reflection dazzles, stuns.

Kuzanagi!

Kuzanagi! the voice of Susano-wu exclaims, echoing off the walls of water as if they were distant mountains. And yet again, Kuzanagi! The errant chamberlain, holding the sword high above his head, parades in a great circle about the circumference of the pit, whence the sound of the wasps feasting still throbs and hums.

Kuzanagi!

Susano-wu speaks to the sword, welcoming it back into the guardianship of his family, apologizing humbly for its loss and captivity in the lair of the serpent-demon. The sword gleams and shimmers as if this were a way of speaking and it were replying to the words of the chamberlain, accepting his homage and praising the victory he has scored over Lord Serpent.

Holding the famous sword above his head, Susano-wu whirls it in a shimmering circle. The light dazzles Kishimo and all those watching. When Susano-wu lowers the sword once more his chamberlain's regalia is replaced by the trappings of a mighty general: he bears the *saihai* baton with flowing tassel of bright horsehair; his helmet carries the peacock feathers of the commander.

Kneeling on the sand, he holds the shimmering sword with

hilt reversed, presses its gleaming tip to his belly and makes a single sweeping stroke, committing honorable *hara-kiri* in his moment of triumph.

No blood spills nor does dying Susano-wu suffer: instead, a brilliance like that of Kuzanagi suffuses his form, he glows like the Mirror of Amaterasu.

From the pit of the monster there is a sound like thunder and there emerges not any of the four great wasps but instead a glistening, flaming beast with hooves of onyx, tail of lightning, wings of fire, terrible face like thunder, and horn as of a narwhal: the *kirin*.

The *kirin* gallops across the sand, kneels before the transfigured Susano-wu. Susano-wu mounts the beast and they rise to the distant heavens, trailing a stream of golden flame behind, disappearing at last into the blinding glow of the sun.

13

The Kishimo rubs her eyes. The monster is dead, the *kirin* that replaced the four giant wasps is gone, carrying upon its back the triumphant Susano-wu. The lost children of the villagers and river-folk of Izumo have been carried away happily to merry-make in houseboats and in huts. Kishimo and Aizen and Okinu-nushi remain alone on the pier over the dry bed of the river Hi.

Yet before them upon the warm sand there lies an object near the dead remains of Lord Serpent. It is a long, glowing blade with lacquered, decorated handle.

Kishimo leaps from pier to sand and runs across the river bed to kneel before the glowing sword Kuzanagi. She reaches one hand toward it timidly, draws back, then reaches again with both hands, clutching the gorgeous hilt of the sword. The hilt is of glistening black lacquer worked with vivid yellow figures.

Still kneeling, Kishimo raises the sword from the sand. She holds its hilt away from herself, moving as if to emulate Susano-wu's deed, but the sword refuses to address itself to her flesh. As if living, it pulls away, pointing toward the Mirror of Amaterasu, drawing Kishimo from her knees so that she stands, sword Kuzanagi raised, sunlight streaming down its blade and filling her body with incomparable joy and power. At length the sword tugs again, and Kishimo, untold, knows that she is to slide it into the scabbard that hangs beneath her *obi*. The *tachi* she had carried earlier is discarded, left to lie on the exposed river bed, to be retrieved by a villager or to remain and rust; in neither case is this longer the concern of Kishimo.

Sheathing the sword—its very entry into Kishimo's scabbard thrills her to every nerve, making her shudder involuntarily with power and pleasure—she becomes aware of two presences beside her on the sand. They are Okinu-nushi the Spirit Master and Aizen-myu. All the others, the villagers, farmers, boatmen, and fishers, have left the scene, pursuing their own affairs in the villages and on the river.

Neither dark Master nor man-god speaks, so Kishimo, left hand clutching the hilt of Kuzanagi, gives voice to wonderment. Our companion is gone, and with Susano-wu the beasts that bore us here. What now, Spirit Master? Can Okinu-nushi summon some shade to guide us?

The dark Master draws himself up, glowing eyes ablaze behind graven mask. His voice, as ever, echoes from within mask and *hoshi-kabuto* as if from a great distance. My power can call any being—but the summoned spirit is not always that which appears. I will summon, Lady. I will summon an earth-sprite of this land of Izumo. We shall learn of our whereabouts and if our fortune is bright we will gain a guide to bring us to Onogoro, the first land of the world.

Lady!

Kishimo nods, makes a small bow of gratitude, remains silent. She steps back from the Spirit Master, as does Aizen-myu.

The Spirit Master Okinu-nushi chants and whirls as he did in the Forest of Ice, the heavens above the land of Izumo turning a dark gray, the warm air growing chill and damp, wind screaming about the ears of Kishimo and the others on the bed of the river Hi. The waters drawn back at the earlier command of the Kanjiu jewel tremble and strain and a heavy spray is torn from them, splattering the three who stand beside the serpent's pit, and yet the walls of water hold their places, the power of the Kanjiu jewel is not overcome by the call of the Spirit Master.

Lady Kishimo! She feels a warm surge within her breast.

Sand-demons stirred by the sudden cold wind rise and dance

about the three, whipping golden pebbles from the river bed and tossing them into the air, scourging Kishimo and Aizen and perhaps even Okinu-nushi. Sand-demons rise and fall, grow and shimmer and dissipate, but some of them remain longer than others, and some begin to show features, limbs and heads and faces, and finally all fall away save one, and the wind slacks although it does not cease, and the churning and whipping of the walled-up river waters grows more steady although it does not cease, and the remaining sand-demon stands whirling in the center of the triangle formed by Kishimo, Aizen-myu, Okinu-nushi.

The Spirit Master stands his ground, his whirling and chanting finished. In a deep but distant voice he speaks: Earth-Sprite! Earth-Sprite! I, the Spirit Master, have raised you from this river bed! I will command your tongue!

The sand-demon dances a full circle about the dark Master, and from within the spinning funnel of sand speaks a voice like that of the earth itself: Spirit Master, fool! Spirit Master, fool! You think I am a sprite of this little place? Behold!

The whirling ceases, the sand falls away, there stands revealed from within a creature like many Kishimo has seen before. In fact, she recognizes the being.

You are the king of the *shikome*, Kishimo cries. You were one whom I met with the Aizen aboard *Ofuna!*

The *shikome* turns to face her. Ai, so you know me! You are a wiser one than this wonder-worker, my lady. I bow before your virtue!

The *shikome*, grotesque parody of a man, makes obeisance before Kishimo, the gnarled king's head lowered and his waist bent, thick hands on his weapons to hold them from jiggling.

Kishimo returns the gesture in like kind. She speaks to the *shikome:* You do me honor, king. He nods. But you give affront to Okinu-nushi the Spirit Master. Kishimo resumes: It was he who drew you here, not I. Why do you speak so to him?

The *shikome* snorts in annoyance. Spirit Master! Demiurge! That one is fit to cure bullocks of the evil eye. And he thinks himself a supreme wonder-worker! He tried to summon a river-sprite or earth-sprite and instead he drew me here. Next he'll try to mend a fisherman's toothache and give the whole village warts instead. Fool!

The being whirls to face Aizen-myu. To him, again, he bows —although not quite as deeply as he did to Kishimo. The woman watches and makes note but offers no comment.

The Aizen returns the bow and speaks: Old friend! Are you pleased to be here? Are you pleased to see me once more? Do not curse the dark Master who called you here. He deserves your gratitude.

At this the *shikome* wrinkles a grotesque lumpy nose but offers no other sign of disagreement.

And since you are here—Aizen asks the creature—what can you tell of *Ofuna* and the infant Miroku?

Ai, ai, a broad grin breaks across the twisted face of the *shikome,* he claps his hands once in glee. *Ofuna!* Miroku! You have been absent from the ship too long, Aizen-myu. Your rival extends his sway. Your followers grow fewer and those of the infant monarch more numerous.

The *shikome* king cackles loudly, clutching his sides with laughter. *Ofuna! Ofuna! Ofuna!* he shouts. Where is the ship, Aizen-myu?

The man-god waits silently for the *shikome* king to subside.

Kishimo, watching and listening, is dizzied by the day and the sunlight beating upon her. All that has happened rushes back to her: the drawing away of the waters of the river Hi, the emergence from its pit of the demon-serpent, the challenge and the strange duel between it and Susano-wu; the chamberlain's strange *hara-kiri* and his ascension on the back of the magical *kirin.* She clutches the rounded and ridged lacquer-decorated hilt of the sword Kuzanagi, passed in its scabbard through her *obi,* and feels comforted.

The Aizen-myu speaks: Where is the ship *Ofuna?*

Very near! the *shikome* cries. Very near! I can go there now. I can take another with me, but only one, man-god. Shall I carry off the lady? Should I let the little trick-worker here ride my back like a child on a wooden horse? Hey, fly, *shikome!*

Carry little peachling where you will! Bring peachling home for milk and rice! Fly, *shikome!*

Again the creature shrieks with glee.

Okinu-nushi, silent throughout the exchanges between the gnarled king and the lady, the gnarled king and the man-god, draws himself upright until he stands taller by a head than any other man. The carven features of his mask grow angry with his frown. The deepset, glowing eyes gleam in fury from beneath the rim of his *hoshi-kabuto.*

Creature! the distant voice echoes and ripples. Creature! It was I who summoned you hence and it is I who banish you from this place! Leave the bed of the river Hi! Depart from the land of Izumo! Go! Go!

The *shikome* quivers, his ragged accounterment streams as if caught in the teeth of a gale, yet Kishimo, standing not a spear's length from the gnarled king, feels no wind at all. The *shikome* leans against the unseen, unfelt stream.

The Spirit Master gestures, gestures, chants.

The *shikome's* feet almost leave the ground. He digs the toes of his claw-tipped, almost-bird-like feet into the sand. Sun and cloud battle for dominance of the sky above.

Little Wizard, I go, the *shikome* shouts to Okinu-nushi. Come you with me, the *shikome* bellows, reaching for the wrist of Aizen-myu. The *shikome's* feet lose their grasp on the loose, whirling sand and he is carried into the air overhead, dragging the Aizen-myu behind him, their clothing streaming out, the voice of the twisted monarch trailing behind as they are swept from overhead and away: Lady Kishimo, we go to *Ofuna* and you and the trick-maker will follow us there, will you or no!

And with a single audible shriek of wind they are gone. The clouds overhead dissipate in an instant. The Mirror of Amaterasu shines brightly upon Kishimo and Okinu-nushi. The woman, Kishimo, is captured by the brilliance of an object lying upon the sand, gleaming roundly in the strong sunlight. Kishimo bends and lifts the object. It is the Nanjiu jewel, the jewel of the rising tide. Left behind by Aizen-myu, by design or by happenstance in the moment of his hasty departure with the *shikome* king. Kishimo now possesses the full pair, Kanjiu and Nanjiu, jewel of the ebbing tide and jewel of the rising tide.

She speaks to the dark Master, Okinu-nushi: Spirit Master, our work here is complete. Susano-wu has reclaimed the honor of his ancient house. The Izumo people have regained their lost children. One monster is destroyed, never again to spread terror beneath heaven.

But still the quest of Miroku and Aizen-myu continues. Still the ship *Ofuna* sails for the land of Tsunu, whether through the Sea of Mists or beyond, and we have yet to find her.

Still, too, we face the oracle spoken by the *shikome* king. We must settle now, what are we to do?

The Spirit Master, metal mask working like a face in indecision, stands swaying before the woman, nearly trembling. You hold the sword Kuzanagi, the dark Master's voice comes at last. You must determine what to do.

Kishimo leaps into the vacant pit that held the eight-headed serpent for so long. Turning back, she sees Okinu-nushi gliding behind her, his feet as ever barely touching the ground over which he passes. Kishimo draws from within her kimono the Nanjiu jewel and raises it, presses it to her brow, commands the waters of the river Hi to return to their ancient bed.

She replaces the jewel in her clothing as the waters rush back into place overhead. Kishimo draws the sword Kuzanagi from its scabbard and a brilliant glow fills the pit, the blade of Kuzanagi gleaming with a light like that of the Mirror of Amaterasu, captured and made small and rendered into the form of a magnificent *tachi* heavily decorated with *horimono* of most ancient deities disporting themselves in the heavens above Onogoro the first land.

Kishimo raises the blade overhead and with it cleaves the solid rock wall of the serpent's pit. The wall opens before the blade of Kuzanagi like a layer of thin cotton before the assault of a fine-honed *tanto* or an *aikuchi* armor piercer.

Kishimo steps through the opening and finds herself in a passageway stretching as far as the eye can see, away, away, away. The passage seems to grow narrower as it proceeds, but

Kishimo, halting to study its course, discerns that this is merely the illusion of narrowing caused by the distance penetrated.

She advances into the passage, sword Kuzanagi raised before her, its brilliant blade gleaming like a pitch-coated torch, yet both more brightly and more steadily than any torch, its constant illumination a green-tinted white that clarifies the rounded, rough stone walls and ceiling and floor of tunnel. Other passageways separate from the main path, leading to chambers and vistas on either hand. Kishimo strides slowly, glancing to each side as she passes, yet neither turning nor pausing at any.

One opening offers the vista of a dense, steaming jungle where tons-heavy dragons bellow and pound, devouring one another, great leather-winged monsters with spear-long jaws and rows of terrifying teeth like *aikuchi* swoop and clack, and carnivorous plants hold up bowls of honey-sweet sap glistening in the sun to trap any unwary passerby.

Another tunnel leads to a realm of blackness where points of starlight glimmer brilliantly and sheets of cosmic dust and powder glow in luminous tints of red and green, yellow and blue; rocks the size of kingdoms flash through emptiness and little flashing specks like arrowheads of fashioned iron flit and fall from starpoint to starpoint.

A bright vista opens upon a city of tall houses towering as high as mountains, men and women more numerous than pine needles in the Forest of Ice tremble and hasten from place to place while heavy machines pound and grind, sparkle and stamp, and men and women suffer life only to enjoy the use of the machines and suffer death in time to meet the needs of the machines.

Another where monsters wear clothing and build temples and worship gods cast up in their own forms.

Another where a neuter figure, black as night, pursues an androgyne, yellow as chrome, across vistas of vacancy and nebulas of dust.

Another where a great city toils beneath a bright sun and clear sky and a single speck drones across the sky and a still tinier speck falls and there is suddenly a second sun glowing and pulsing in the air and the city is in an instant reduced to heaps of stinking, smoldering rubble.

Now, far ahead, Kishimo sees a figure in *kabuto* helmet and *tanko* old-style iron armor, with a tall *naga-suyari* spear, the strong straight-bladed spear resembling an oversized *yanagi-ba* arrow in one hand. Kishimo approaches more closely and sees that the figure is a mere wooden rack holding armor, helmet, and spear.

The armor is strong and gracefully cast, tied with yellow silk.

The spear is of smooth lacquered wood, its plum-leaf *naga-suyari* blade bound to a cleft in the wood with matching yellow silk cord.

The *kabuto* helmet is most odd of all: formed like a conch-shell war trumpet, the mouthpiece of the trumpet making the *tehen* hole, the small opening at the peak of the helmet; in lieu of crest or decoration the helmet bears a stylized iron *nigiryu no kabuto*, a sculpted fist grasping a heavenly thunderbolt as if to hurl it at a battle foe.

As Okinu-nushi the Spirit Master stands by, Kishimo lifts *tanko* armor from its wooden rack and dons it over her kimono and breeches, shifting the sword Kuzanagi as she needs to, strapping its scabbard to the *tanko* cuirass; she places the *nigiryu no kabuto* with its fist and thunderbolt firmly over her headband, the helmet's neck protector covering her dark hair. At last she removes the plum-leaf-blade spear, *naga-suyari,* from its place and fixes it onto her iron-plate cuirass, where it can be removed at need.

The tunnel here ends; Kishimo, using the *naga-suyari* spear rather than the shining sword Kuzanagi, casts blade at wall. By its own power the spear returns to Kishimo, its lacquered haft settling as a bird on the arm of its master, into her hand. Where the plum-leaf blade had struck the tunnel end there opens a new passage, a winding walkway leading upward; the walls and roof of the walkway are of raw earth. Roots of trees from above appear in the walls, and creepers dangle from overhead. The path underfoot is paved with tinted oblong sections of glazed porcelain. No speck of dust nor track of traveler mars the glossy surface; it is as if the passageway has come into being with the cast of the *naga-suyari,* and Kishimo and Okinu-nushi are the first beings ever to tread its length.

Turning and casting back her eyes, Kishimo sees the dark Spirit Master following her, and behind him the pathway they trod slowly closing up again, leaving behind them a wall of fresh earth, moist and fecund and dark.

A third time Kishimo and Okinu-nushi confront a blockage to their progress. This time it is a great ornate polished oval, a mirror in which Kishimo sees herself, resplendent in warrior's gear, *nigiryu no kabuto, tanko do* bound with yellow silk, *naga-suyari* spear and sword Kuzanagi; and beside her, tall and masked, eyes glowing beneath *kabuto,* the Spirit Master Okinu-nushi.

To the touch of Kishimo's spear the mirror offers no response; even to the scintillant Kuzanagi the mirror yields nothing. Kishimo sheathes sword, fixes spear to *tanko do* cuirass. She reaches beneath her cuirass, draws forth both Nanjiu and Kanjiu jewels, and holding them before her in either hand, entreats the mirror to permit passage to herself and the Master.

The silvery surface shimmers and pales. Kishimo steps forward, followed by Okinu-nushi. They find themselves once more at the edge of the sea, facing a glittering green-blue surface. The sky above is as blue as porcelain, as clear as fine glass; the sun is white and tiny and its rays strong. A fresh breeze whips wavelets against rocky shore, snapping little sheets of spray into the air and carrying them inland the short distance to Kishimo and Okinu-nushi.

Before them the sea stretches to a sharp, curving horizon dotted with white puffs of cotton; behind them a sparse stand of iron-tough timber clings fiercely to a jagged landscape.

Now I must act, the Spirit Master says, his voice as ever echoing from behind sculpted lips as from a great distance. You have brought us here, Lady. I must carry us onward. But to do this I must borrow your long spear.

Carefully Kishimo unlooses the *naga-suyari* weapon from her iron *do* cuirass. *Tsuba* guard foremost, she passes the weapon to Okinu-nushi; the lacquered hilt feels as warm as flesh in her hands, reluctant to part from her grasp.

Yet once gripped by the dark Spirit Master, the *naga-suyari* quiets, awaiting the command of a new lord.

The Spirit Master climbs the steep hillside from the sea to the stand of gnarled, tough trees growing above. As ever, his gliding feet seem barely to touch the earth. He halts before a tall pine and bows his helmeted head; Kishimo hears the Master's tones as he prays to the tall pine.

As if from the bright, distant sun itself, a small bird flutters downward, chirping a cry and searching for some object of interest only to creatures of its own kind. The bird, silhouetted blackly against the Mirror of Amaterasu, swoops over the heads of the travelers, rising again to an upper limb of the tall pine; at the lowest point in the bird's course its wings open to drive it upward again and Kishimo sees its symmetrical markings of bright chrome-yellow feathers.

The bird hovers for a moment, beating its wings rapidly, then settles upon a high limb. A cracking sound, low yet sharp, echoes from the rocky hillsides and a small, hard object topples from the limb, bounding and tumbling off lower and lower branches as it falls. At last it strikes the earth and rolls to a halt before the still-humbled Spirit Master. With a final expression of gratitude to the tree itself and to the sun goddess Amaterasu for dispatching her messenger, Okinu-nushi kneels, lifts the fallen pine cone in one hand as he holds the *naga-suyari* spear in the other, and glides rapidly to the edge of the land.

Here he kneels once again, and using the plum-shaped blade of the spear as his tool, strips a single strobilus from the deodar. Murmuring over the strobilus, Okinu-nushi sets it carefully aside and strips another from the cone, and another, until the deodar cone is reduced to a single twig-like core rod.

Okinu-nushi sets the rod upright on the mossy soil, ranges the stripped-away strobili about it, and utters a chant, stroking the chip-like strobili all the while with Kishimo's *naga-suyari* spear. The chips distend and affix themselves to the rod; the rod in its turn grows taller and thicker. From the tall deodar pine a feather flutters downward, graceful and yellow. It lands softly in the hand of Kishimo, who fixes it to the upright wooden rod.

Their craft completed, Kishimo and Okinu-nushi launch their cockleshell upon the sparkling water, Kishimo once more armed with sword and spear. At the command of Okinu-nushi, wind-spirites arise from the sea and propel the raft forward, the single yellow feather billowing and growing before the wind into a great snapping sail.

The black-and-yellow bird leaves its perch high in the deodar pine and circles over the rapidly moving raft until the island is a small speck abaft, then arrows away once more.

Kishimo and Okinu-nushi continue across sparkling waters in silence, the wind-sprites propelling their feather-sailed raft before them, the only sound being the snapping of the sail and the lappings of fresh sparkling wavelets against the strobilus-planked raft.

Slowly the sun descends, slowly the day lengthens, until at last it is dusk. The raft sails steadily onward, coursing into the golden cloud-gloried horizon, when a form appears once more silhouetted dead ahead against the background of the glowing Mirror.

Masts and sails, castles and decks, dark woods and glowing lanterns; Kishimo at once recognizes and turns to see if the Spirit Master also knows the object that bobs softly in the sea before the feather-sail raft. His helmet lowers and raises, dark shadow beneath and glowing eyes smoky and great.

Okinu-nushi too knows that they approach *Ofuna*.

14

The Mirror of Amaterasu sinks into the eastern sea; a final flare
of crimson and the sun disappears. As if at the hands of ten
myriad lamplighters at once, the stars spring into the heaven,
constellations burning against the black pit of the endless upper
realm.

There is no moon.

Aboard *Ofuna,* lanterns swing from spars and lighted cabins
glow through portholes. The cockleshell bearing Kishimo and
Okinu-nushi is plunged into darkness; rather than draw the
sword Kuzanagi once more and use its effulgence for their
illumination, Kishimo asks Okinu-nushi to summon a
lantern-sprite.

The dark Spirit Master gestures flippantly with one armored
finger, mutters a few low syllables; a point of brilliance appears
overhead and settles atop the pine-reed mast of the cockleshell.
Wind-sprites push the raft onward until it nestles against the tall
hull of *Ofuna.* Sailors watching the approach of the tiny boat
by force of the bobbing flicker atop its mast cast lines over the
side of *Ofuna* and Okinu-nushi grasps them.

The wind- and lantern-sprites are dismissed and the feather
sail of the little craft shrivels back to a single yellow bird-pin;
the planks and mast of the boat draw back upon themselves
and as Kishimo and Okinu-nushi draw themselves up the
knotted lines to the deckrail of *Ofuna,* a deodar pine cone and

fluffy feather drift away, slowly bobbing on the wavelets of the calmly lapping sea.

The two travelers set foot on the ship's deck to find themselves surrounded by sailors. An officer of the night watch approaches and stares for a moment at the newcomers, then bows deeply before them. He has never before seen the Spirit Master but knows of him from tales. His appearance is one of fear. He has seen Kishimo before, during her prior sojourn aboard *Ofuna,* but he pauses briefly as if uncertain of her person; then the watch officer bows more deeply in awe of the woman.

Kishimo and Okinu-nushi bow in return.

You will take us to your master Miroku, Kishimo commands the officer. Once more he bows and leads them through clustering sailors who appear from darkened sectors of the deck to peer at the armed and armored lady and the demiurge Okinu-nushi. They reach the castle of the ship and duck their heads to prevent the tall crest of Okinu-nushi's helmet, the fist and thunderbolt of Kishimo's, from catching against the high beam.

The watch officer bows Master and Lady through the entryway of the baffle that admits them to the luxurious cabin of Miroku. They stand before the infant monarch's gold-hung throne; he observes them through large dark eyes that glitter in the flickering light of lanterns.

Kishimo bows low.

Okinu-nushi bows low.

Miroku, on his carven throne, rich gown of gold and turquoise sparkling in lanternlight, inclines his head.

The air is scented with the presence of crushed blossoms and burnt incense.

Miroku, with an idle gesture of his chubby, child-like hand, indicates cushions for Kishimo and Okinu-nushi, and they seat themselves upon them, maintaining a respectful silence until the monarch and captain of *Ofuna* should initiate a discourse. At length Miroku, with the smile of a happy infant and the eyes of an ancient, does so.

Spirit Master, welcome aboard *Ofuna*. We have never met but your fame is widespread. You are most welcome.

Okinu-nushi bows his thanks.

Kishimo, Miroku resumes. Perhaps now best called the Lady Kishimo—you have earned such respectful address.

Kishimo bows.

I have received reports and observations of your travels, my Lady Kishimo, Miroku pipes. Despite his high childish tones, his delivery is portentous. I have followed you from my ship to the raider in the Sea of Mists, thence to the land of Yomi, to the island of the Forest of Ice, to the land of Izumo and the river Hi, and through your return to *Ofuna*.

I see that you who left with only kimono and *obi*, with *eboshi* to cushion your temples, return with thunderbolt *kabuto*, *tanko* armor, plum-leaf-blade spear, and the famous sword Kuzanagi. You have traveled far and learned much, my Lady Kishimo. You are fitted now to join me in the great exploit of taking the land of Tsunu.

And you, Spirit Master, continues Miroku, if you would give your aid to my forces, you would be most welcome in your adventure.

From beneath the helm of Okinu-nushi's *kabuto*, eyes glow deeply, gleaming in the low-lit cabin of Miroku; from the molded lips of his metal mask the Spirit Master's voice echoes as from a distant mountainside. It would please me to join you, Miroku, Lord Miroku, and the Lady Kishimo. I too have learned. I doubt that you would need my powers in your adventure, but they are at your disposal should you find use for them.

Miroku thanks the dark Master.

And the Aizen-myu? Kishimo asks.

He too has returned to *Ofuna*, Miroku replies. He is in the cavern of the *shikome* along with those servants of his will. He rallies his demon followers for the assault upon Tsunu, the object of all our efforts.

Kishimo ponders. Of all the men and gods she has

encountered, Aizen-myu has proven the most changeable. Friend and foe, foe and friend, and finally, from the serpent's pit beneath the bed of the river Hi, one who willingly departed with his *shikome* companion. The act was not one of treason, yet it was not one bespeaking loyalty or steadfastness by any means.

To Miroku, Kishimo says: Have you faith in the purpose of the Aizen-myu?

The infant monarch beams and nods. That have I, my Lady Kishimo.

You have seen him in the cavern of the *shikome* at his end of the ship? persists Kishimo. You have seen, you know what he does there with his odd band of retainers?

That I do not, Miroku responds. Neither magical vision nor mundane spies have I in the camp of the Aizen-myu. Nor, as far as I know, has the Aizen here among my own followers. But that I do not know for a certainty either.

Kishimo turns to Okinu-nushi the Spirit Master. Can you gather this wisdom for us, Spirit Master? Can you see into the cavern of the *shikome* where the Aizen tarries now?

The dark Okinu-nushi turns his head to one side, then to the other, as a mortal would sign his denial, but with a ponderousness unlike that of any man.

Is there no way we can find out what is happening there? asks Kishimo, persisting. Could you summon some spirit and send it to spy on the Aizen? Could you summon the spirit of one of his *shikome* to you? Or the spirit of the Aizen-myu himself?

No, Lady, I could never summon up the spirit of the Aizen-myu himself, for he is a greater being than I, and the power of spirit-summoning is so made that only the greater may call up the lesser, never the lesser the greater, save by the will of the greater, which surely Aizen-myu would not yield to me.

Nor could I summon a spirit and send it to the *shikome* cavern to spy. For, once sent, a spirit goes where it wills. And as for calling a *shikome* from the cavern—that I could do, but I could not compel it to speak truthfully. Thus its report would be worse than worthless, for we would have word that might be true or that might be dissimulation contrived for the very end of misdirecting our efforts.

Kishimo remains unmoving, pondering further. The ship *Ofuna,* graceful wooden craft with tall masts and slatted bamboo sails square-rigged to capture a following breeze, rocks gently in the night sea. The baffle at the entryway of Miroku's cabin holds off distracting light and sound from the companionways and decks of the ship, but through an open porthole comes the lulling sound of water lapping at *Ofuna's* hull, the occasional splash of a leaping fish. This is not the Sea of Mists but a warmer and pleasanter sea altogether.

As *Ofuna* rocks in gentle swells, the lantern flames that illumine the cabin dance and cast swerving shadows of the demiurge, the infant monarch, the armor-clad woman.

You may send me, Spirit Master, for I am woman and you are more than a human creature, and further I would yield to you my will for the sending. I will spy out the cavern of Aizen-myu and return here. Send me, Spirit Master.

The echoing voice says: I am far from certain now that you are any lesser being than I, my Lady Kishimo. But as you consent to my sending, even then it may be done.

I do consent, she says.

Kishimo's eye is caught for an instant by the infant Miroku, but the fat-cheeked, jolly-baby, wise-eyed Miroku does not speak. His glance is piercing but it is enigmatic. Does it say, Proceed? Does it say, Hold? Kishimo wishes she could fathom the message, but she does not speak her question, and Miroku's wordless advice is beyond her understanding.

I do consent.

The dark Master swells and rises, his dragon-crested *hoshi-kabuto,* starry helmet, soars as if to crash against the ceiling, but the beams are themselves lost in lofty darkness. The flickering lanterns in the swaying cabin grow dim. The glittering jeweled kimono of the infant Miroku flashes faintly and lapses into darkness.

Only the glowing coals of Okinu-nushi's eyes, radiating from deep behind his wrought-metal face, give illumination. Kishimo gazes into those eyes, raising her head ever higher as the Spirit Master swells and rises, swells and rises above her.

As if pressed down by an unseen force, Kishimo sinks to her knees on the deck of Miroku's cabin, holding her head upright and tilted back so that her eyes stay locked on those of Okinu-nushi. She sees two great objects rising from beside Okinu-nushi and wonders what they could be: great war dogs, fierce dark-winged hawks—and then she realizes that they are his hands, fingers extended and working in mystical passes.

The distant, echoing voice of the Spirit Master rises in chant.

Kishimo feels herself growing light, rising, rising as if lifted by the gestures of those hands, yet they do not touch her. She rises to the level of the dark Master's hands, to the level of his *do-maru* armored cuirass, to the level of those hot, glowing eyes.

Her mind is filled with the sound of Okinu-nushi's chanting; at the twining of his hands in their mystical configurations she feels herself revolving slowly, gazing downward from a great height of darkness in the cabin of the Miroku.

Only the Spirit Master's glowing eyes accompany her, and yet she can look downward and observe him still, can see the top of his star helmet: the sculpted metal dragon crest writhes and glares up at her, its eyes the same glowing coals as the Master's; the dragon's mouth opens and rushes of brilliant flame pour upward at her. They pass around her on all sides but cause her no pain.

She sees the form of a woman kneeling before the Spirit Master.

She hears the chanting of the Master, and now as never before its meaning is clear to her, guiding her, sustaining her as she moves effortlessly through space, through the bulkheads and decks of *Ofuna,* past sailors, past lanterns, penetrating ever toward the far end of the ship, penetrating ever deeper beneath the water line, and at length she finds herself hovering high in the great cavern of the *shikome* where clusters of the grotesque near-human figures gather and sway about gouts of flame that rise from a rocky floor.

From a far corner of the cavern she hears voices in dialogue, one angry and commanding, the other mocking and laughing.

Kishimo floats across the roof of the cavern, passing stalactites and mold-crusted fissures from which slow trickles of chilly water dribble. She hovers above a violet flame where Ibaraki, king of the *shikome*, confronts the man-god Aizen-myu.

Ibaraki holds his *naginata* lance, tossing it from hand to hand carelessly as he mocks the Aizen. Ibaraki, whose one hand is of the weird flesh of the *shikome* and whose other hand, lost to the sword stroke of Yorimutsu's *katani* sword, is of *tekko* metal workmanship. The lance striking his hand of flesh makes a soft thump; striking his hand of iron, it makes a harsh clanking sound.

Thus: thump, *clank,* thump, *clank.*

Kishimo hovers, watching and listening.

Aizen-myu is demanding the aid and obedience of the *shikome* bands as a battery of marines to attack and subdue all of the ship not under his control. Miroku must be conquered, and after the conquest of Miroku, *Ofuna* will be sailed to the land of Tsunu, where Aizen's overwhelming forces will dispose of the present rulers and establish Aizen-myu as emperor.

One-handed Ibaraki has no interest in Tsunu, cares for *Ofuna* only to carry himself and his people the *shikome* to their own homeland, Onogoro.

After Tsunu is taken, Aizen-myu appeases, after Miroku is overcome and Tsunu recovered, *Ofuna* will sail once again and the *shikome* will return to Onogoro. Ibaraki, king of the *shikome,* will reign in Onogoro.

Ibaraki laughs unpleasantly.

Aizen-myu's countenance shows great anger.

The *shikome* laughs the louder, dancing and mocking.

The Aizen, shouting, draws *tachi* longsword and menaces Ibaraki.

The grotesque monarch hurls one hand to grasp the

horimono-engraved swordblade. The blade is far beyond the reach of Ibaraki's arm but the iron *tekko* hand, flung with great power, separates from the *shikome*'s fleshy wrist and strikes the Aizen's blade, resounding as an iron clapper in a silver bell, with a mixture of the harsh and the sweet, sending a flare of sparks into the air whence they shower upon man-god and manling equally, bouncing from armor and arcing to stone cavern floor.

Again the *shikome* Ibaraki laughs unpleasantly.

The quarrel continues; Kishimo hovers above the two disputants, uncertain as to her concealment should she lower herself to their level. She watches fascinated as Ibaraki's *tekko* iron hand returns to his wrist and he brandishes Aizen's longsword between them.

Aizen, raging, demands the return of his weapon and Ibaraki, disdainful, turns the sword hilt-uppermost and tosses it high to the taller Aizen. The man-god turns his eyes toward the roof of the cavern, following the flight of the sword. He catches the sword by its hilt and stands gazing upward, eyes fixed on Kishimo.

She trembles, awaiting his action.

He looks puzzled, deep furrows creasing the flesh of his forehead beneath the rim of his own *kabuto*. Then, still puzzled, he returns to his dispute, sheathing his longsword as one ashamed.

Kishimo hears a sound like the wind on a distant peak, like the chant of a distant monk; she feels herself drawn swiftly and resistlessly away from the scene of the dispute. In a wink she is back in the cabin of the infant Miroku, gazing down upon the Spirit Master and upon her own kneeling form. She drops past the glowering dragon helm, past the hot-eyed masked face, finds herself unsteadily rising from her knees. She stumbles forward and catches at the lacing of the elaborate *do-maru* cuirass. She feels the hands of the Spirit Master on her shoulders, holding her upright, steadying her against vertigo.

Good, a piping voice sounds. You return safely, Kishimo.

She turns toward the sound. It is the infant ruler Miroku.

Kishimo bows to each in turn, Okinu-nushi and Miroku. She tells what she has seen and heard.

My dear colleague, Miroku pipes. Quickly, can we prevent this battle for control of *Ofuna?* Okinu-nushi—what says the Master?

Can you muster a superior force, Miroku?

The reedy piping: Not so quickly. My forces are spread about *Ofuna,* tending to rigging and hull, deck and cabins and hold. They can match the *shikome* of Aizen but not before the *shikome* overcome our sector of the ship. But can you not summon spirits to combat the *shikome,* Okinu-nushi?

Spirits best confront spirits, Miroku, the dark Master replies. Whom I could summon, could not overcome the bands of *shikome* mustered by Ibaraki in league with the Aizen.

There is a *crack!* as the butt of Kishimo's spear strikes angrily the hardwood deck beside a soft carpet in Miroku's cabin. The woman's left hand clenches about the shaft of the polished-lacquer spear shaft and her right hand flies involuntarily to close on the hilt of the sword Kuzanagi, still thrust along with its scabbard through her *obi,* fixed to her iron cuirass.

Quarrel! Quarrel! Kishimo explodes. Chatter while your rival prepares to attack! I will confront the *shikome.* I will not kill Aizen, for he has been my friend and he has saved my life but I will prevent the *shikome* from taking *Ofuna,* and then we shall see what is what!

Not waiting for comment from Miroku or Okinu-nushi, the woman dodges her way through the baffle separating the cabin of Miroku from the companionway outside, and races, spear and sword hilt clutched in either hand, toward the cabin of the *shikome.*

At the portal of the long descent leading to the cavern she confronts a short, hairy *shikome* climbing, knife held in crooked teeth, from the cavern onto the deck of *Ofuna.* Kishimo swings the butt of her spear at the *shikome,* knocking him head over heels, tumbling into a row of companions who follow.

More *shikome* advance. The woman Kishimo glances behind her, sees sailors gathering, officers shouting, milling and confusion, but she has no time to observe. She turns back, stands facing the portal of the *shikome* cavern. She must make a stand here, she realizes: to step back will permit an outrush of the Onogoro demons and the overwhelming of the ship; to step forward places her among a horde of her foes. But if she can remain fighting in the portal she can face *shikome* singly or in small enough numbers to triumph over.

A second charge comes at her, little better organized than the first. There is daylight behind her and distant fire flares within the cavern. Two *shikome* tumble up the companionway to attack Kishimo; again she uses the butt of her spear against one, sending him reeling backward, first jostling his companion and knocking him off balance. Before the second attacker can regain himself, Kishimo jabs at him with the plum-leaf-shaped blade of her spear and the demon in dodging its double-edged tip loses balance completely and falls away from the confrontation.

Another demon comes at Kishimo now. Over the head of the squat, ugly creature Kishimo can see the king of the demons, Ibaraki, gesturing and screaming at his minions to break past Kishimo and take the ship, but Kishimo jabs with her spear, gripping it tightly in both her *yugake*-gloved hands. The *shikome* opens its hideously fanged mouth to shriek its battlecry at Kishimo—and another jab of her spear, designed to force the *shikome* into a battle-losing leap, instead penetrates the palate of the demon. With a gout of red-black blood the creature topples backward and tumbles away.

Now Ibaraki, furious, shoulders through his minions, shoving them to left and right, bulling to the head of the companionway to confront Kishimo. *Ai!* the demon king shouts, this is the lady of the river Hi. Here you have no chamberlain of Yomi to conquer in your behalf, Lady. Here you shall go down to defeat.

No words from Kishimo. She tightens her grasp on her spear and lunges at Ibaraki's face, intending not the same fatal probe as against her last opponent, but to drive the demon king off balance. He dodges easily, moving his head aside on a surprisingly supple neck; Kishimo's spear blade slides harmlessly off the side of the *shikome* king's *kabuto.*

The *shikome,* armed also with long-hafted spear, drives its tip at the chest of Kishimo. She attempts to dodge but the blade strikes her *do-maru,* metal cuirass bound with yellow silk. The blade does not penetrate the cuirass but its impact staggers Kishimo. In an instant Ibaraki will be through the portal, followed by a horde of *shikome;* this Kishimo cannot permit. She drives herself forward once more, sees the point of Ibaraki's spear loom before her face, ducks quickly.

The blade passes between her cheek and the inner lining of her *hoshi-kabuto;* both Kishimo and Ibaraki draw back at the same moment, the demon's blade drawing a long, shallow line along Kishimo's cheek; she sees her own blood splash from beneath her *kabuto,* staining the yellow silk bindings of her *do-maru.* Shocked, she stands with spear gripped before her, and again the *shikome* lunges, crying now in triumph.

Kishimo deflects his blow with the haft of her spear, recovers, smashes downward with the butt of her lance, using her advantage of height and placement. The spear crashes against the crown of Ibaraki's helmet, sending splinters of sharp sensation up Kishimo's arms. The *shikome* staggers now. Kishimo follows with an upward blow of her spear butt, aiming it to strike Ibaraki's face beneath his helm. She succeeds in part: the blow lands on the visoredge of the *kabuto* and Ibaraki's spear is raised across his chest in a defensive posture.

Kishimo slashes with the plum-leaf-shaped blade of her lance. Ibaraki raises his spear higher, deflecting the blow, but the power of Kishimo's slash knocks the spear from the *shikome* king's grasp. The spear topples away toward the floor of the cavern; Kishimo and Ibaraki, standing in frozen tableau, strain to hear its clatter. For eternities there is only silence, and then the distant clash of wood and metal against rock echoes up from the remote cavern floor.

The *shikome* king is jolted back into motion. His *naginata* spear lost to him, facing an opponent holding her own lance at the ready, rather than drawing a shorter blade, the *shikome* hurls his iron *tekko* hand once more. The hand, like a living creature, seizes the spear from Kishimo's surprised grasp and returns with it to Ibaraki's wrist. The demon monarch emits a screech of triumph.

Kishimo, undaunted, reaches to the decorated scabbard hanging from her *obi*. With a smooth sound of polished metal and lacquered wood the sword Kuzanagi leaps from its home and into the hands of the armored woman. Kishimo grasps the sword in both her hands; its polished, *horimono*-graven blade gleams with an inner light that illumines both Kishimo and her opponent Ibaraki. Far beyond the *shikome* leader and his horde of followers Kishimo sees the man-god Aizen calmly observing the battle. For the most fleeting portion of an eye flicker the gaze of the woman and that of the demigod catch, then release once again.

Ibaraki grunts and lunges forward with Kishimo's own spear held grasped in his two hands, one of iron, one of demon-flesh.

Kishimo, reacting, sweeps the sword Kuzanagi through the air, easily deflecting the lunge of Ibaraki. The passage of the sword through the air is like that of a thunderbolt falling from the heavens to the storm-riven earth: a jagged, dancing line of dazzling, fascinating brilliance. Ibaraki easily recovers his posture of readiness but then stands, like Kishimo, staring at the line of light left by the passage of Kuzanagi.

Again Ibaraki lunges and again Kishimo parries. This time her sweep is in the line of her foe's shoulders rather than one slashing from roof to floor; the jagged brilliance cuts that remaining from the prior parry and there remains a glowing, irregular cross in the air. Another lunge and another parry, from shoulder to hip, and the glowing object becomes a six-pointed *hoshi,* star.

Kishimo settles into an easy style of fighting, not bothering to attack her opponent but slowly, steadily weaving a cloth of glowing force lines across the mouth of the cavern. The *shikome* king in growing anger and frustration screams and lunges again and again with his lance, yet to no effect. Finally he lets his lance drop to the floor beneath his feet. In the moment of tacit truce between himself and Kishimo he reaches forward with his *tekko* hand. A bolt of force leaps from the woven screen to the iron claws. Ibaraki howls in pain and jerks back his hand.

Kishimo sheaths the sword Kuzanagi, reaches with one *yugake*-clad hand and touches the lines of light. She feels a tingling run up and down her arm, filling her body with a strange energy.

Shikome soldiers cluster around the cavern side of the woven screen, several touching it carefully with fingertip or weapon. All draw back quickly, many of them dancing and howling as they do so.

In the distance Kishimo sees the Aizen-myu smile strangely, turn away, and disappear into gloom. Kishimo laughs, turns also, strides through *Ofuna* to the cabin of Miroku.

15

In the luxurious chamber of the infant monarch Miroku, Kishimo catches her breath, bows before the suspended throne where the splendidly gowned man-child nods and smiles benignly. You did well, Miroku's shrill voice comes. You grow, Kishimo. You learn. You become strong. Good!

Okinu-nushi, towering and dark as ever, astonishingly bows before Kishimo. Flustered, she responds in like manner.

And now? And now, Kishimo asks, what is our course?

There is a moment of silence in the cabin, then Miroku clenches a fat fist, points a stubby baby finger. To Tsunu! he commands.

Spirit Master! Miroku turns his fat-cheeked face, his old-looking eyes, toward the dark towering figure. Spirit Master! It is my wish that the ship *Ofuna* carry her sailors now to the land of Tsunu. And it is my wish to rise above the ship so that I may survey the progress of our quest. What will you do for me?

Okinu-nushi bows before the tiny ruler. Miroku, the remote voice echoes, Lord Miroku, provide me with any bit of wood and tools with which to build. My Lady Kishimo, the Master turns toward her, if you will give me the use of the sword Kuzanagi, I can accomplish this task.

No, Spirit Master, Miroku commands, the Lady Kishimo has seen your skill in practice. Let her perform the act herself.

The dark Master bows. As Lord Miroku wishes.

The infant points to a *bonsai* deodar resting upon a

decorative lacquered stand. Use this, he commands.

As Okinu-nushi strides to remove a pine cone the size of a housecat's eye from the deodar pine, Kishimo asks Miroku of the fate of Aizen-myu and the *shikome* demons of Ibaraki.

Have no concern over them, Miroku responds. You have bound them so they cannot overrun the rest of *Ofuna,* but there are other ways from their cavern, and the Aizen, for all his ill will toward me, will join us in the conquest of Tsunu. What becomes of him afterward—and of us, my Lady Kishimo —remains to be seen. But I have no doubt that we will see the Aizen, the *shikome,* Lord Ibaraki—all in the land of Tsunu.

Kishimo bows her head, accepting the words of Miroku. She turns once more and sees that Okinu-nushi has removed a single tiny cone from the miniature deodar pine, bowing now before the *bonsai* tree and asking its forgiveness for the removal of its part.

The lanterns illuminating the cabin of Miroku flicker as the ship *Ofuna* rolls slightly; the flickering light makes the *bonsai* bow . . . or seem to bow in response to Okinu-nushi's courtesy.

Okinu-nushi, towering above Kishimo, holds two dark and armored hands before the woman. From the cold hands Kishimo gently lifts the tiny deodar pine cone. She places it with utmost care on the carpeted floor before the throne of Miroku. She draws the sword Kuzanagi slowly, carefully, and its light outshines that of the flickering lanterns in the cabin.

Tenderly Kishimo removes the strobili, laying each carefully beside the central rod of the cone on the carpet. When she is done she uses Kuzanagi carefully to carve the strobili and rod into the parts of a war chariot. When the task is completed, Kishimo sheathes her sword and lifts the chariot, no longer than the pommel of an armor piercer, before the hanging throne of Miroku.

Miroku nods approval, reaches with a gold-and-jewel-decked hand to lift an exquisite toy from the lap of his kimono. Kishimo looks closely: it is a *kirin* carved of multicolored jade, the dragon-horse of the Nether Distant Land. The work is of incomparable fineness and care: every hair, every scale, every claw of the mystic beast is present and perfect.

At Miroku's command Kishimo places the miniature war chariot beside the tiny *kirin*. Miroku passes his hand over the chariot and beast. Kishimo waits to see what will result, but nothing, for the moment, is discerned. Surely the miniature chariot and *kirin* remain, perfect but motionless, before her eyes.

And yet Kishimo turns to observe Okinu-nushi and sees that the dark Master, while as great in stature as ever by the gauge of her own slender form, is shrinking against the spars and hangings and cushions of the Miroku's cabin. Okinu-nushi is growing smaller, and so also is the infant Miroku, although less rapidly, and as the Miroku grows tiny, his baby's proportions are altered into the shape and proportions of an older boy, a young man, a warrior. And Kishimo herself shrinks, shrinks, shrinks.

Finally they cease growing smaller. Kishimo looks at the chariot and at the magical *kirin*. To the size of the three, these are of normal dimensions.

Okinu-nushi? says Kishimo. What question she intended to ask, the woman herself does not know. Merely to seek reassurance from the Spirit Master.

My Lady Kishimo, the echoing voice comes. I am with you.

Lord Miroku, says Kishimo to the little monarch.

Lord Miroku no longer, he utters. Lord Miroku no longer but —Issun Boshi.

Issun Boshi!

Little One Inch!

Miroku no longer, the infant ruler is transformed into the tiny hero of old times. He leaps to the reins of the chariot, calls to Okinu-nushi and Kishimo to bow to him, and no sooner have they obeyed than Issun Boshi calls up the *kirin* to the gallop. The dragon-horse leaps forward, straining its traces, drawing the war chariot behind.

With a strong leap the *kirin* flies into the air, lifting the war chariot, Issun Boshi, Kishimo, and Okinu-nushi with itself. The magical beast circles the royal cabin once, breathing smoke and trailing sparks that bound from the armor of the three riders in the chariot, then plunges through the open porthole of the cabin, charges through a low sheet of sea spray, and rises, circling once again, into the air above the ship *Ofuna*.

At the command of Issun Boshi, Little One Inch, the Spirit Master Okinu-nushi summons up a covey of wind elementals to propel *Ofuna* across the breast of the tranquil sea to the shores of Tsunu.

I have used my powers greatly, Okinu-nushi announces. Now I am weakened, but I will recover.

Such is well, Issun Boshi states.

Kishimo looks closely at the old-time hero known as Little One Inch. Issun Boshi is a man, not a babe like Miroku, yet his eyes contain little of the ancient weariness of the infant ruler. Issun Boshi has the flashing dark-eyed look of strong youth; Okinu-nushi the glowing coal-eyed look of the demiurge. Kishimo wonders about herself, wishes that she could use the Mirror of Amaterasu as a reflecting glass and see her own woman's face.

The chariot flies through the air behind the magical *kirin;* the ship *Ofuna*, far below, proceeds, propelled by wind elementals obeying the will of the Spirit Master. They travel onward with the speed of the wind, yet the distance across the sea to the coast of the land of Tsunu is so great that dusk has fallen before the shoreline heaves into sight.

Ahead of the flying chariot, low waves break on the coast of Tsunu. The shoreline is a study in contrasts: sand as pale and white as the sea foam that rolls up its slope, and rocks as tall as palaces, as sharp as armor-piercing dirks, as black as midnight heavens, make a pattern of jagged streaks. Beyond the beach the countryside of Tsunu stretches away, climbing steadily into row upon row of hills until there rises a rampart of snow-ringed mountains and volcanic cones glowing a dark and angry crimson against the ceiling of distant clouds that float above.

Kishimo holds firmly to the railing that surmounts the war-walls of the flying chariot, turning her gaze behind, to the west, where the Mirror of Amaterasu hovers barely above the brink of the sea, then drops like a sudden plumb below the horizon. The sky in an instant glows red, red-orange rays of the Mirror fan out in promise of another day, then disappear, leaving behind a blackness dotted with uncountable winking stars and tiny floating cloudlets.

The ship *Ofuna,* speeding below the chariot, is visible only by the specks of her lanterns swinging from spars where bamboo sails and cloth sails belly out before the wind elementals' force.

Look now, cries Issun Boshi, pointing to the beach of Tsunu.

Ahead of the chariot and far below it Kishimo can see scores of figures, hundreds of figures swarming on the beach and the rocks.

Little One Inch laughs loud and heartily: a laugh not of bitterness or scorn is rare in Kishimo's experience; this is one of pure amusement. See! Little One Inch points and laughs again. See! It is Aizen-myu, Ibaraki, the *shikome* horde!

Kishimo leans over the railing of the chariot and peers into the darkness, into the distance. The beach is filled with struggling forms, and they are illuminated by bonfires licking upward from the white sands with tongues of crimson and orange. Kishimo hears the distant sound of cries, wails, shouts; clash of metal weapons on metal armor; twang of bowstrings, whiz of arrows.

The attackers are the *shikome* minions of Ibaraki and Aizen-myu; the defenders are the foemen of Issun Boshi, holding this land, this Tsunu, against the invaders.

As the *kirin*-drawn chariot circles slowly overhead, Kishimo watches the progress of the battle. The defenders are ordinary samurai armed with sword, dagger, spear, and bow. The attackers carry similar weapons but are demons, the demon-men of Onogoro, and their rush cannot be resisted. Slowly the lines of the defenders crumble, slowly their numbers diminish.

There is no withdrawal from this battle, but a constant

abrasion of the line of defenders against the mass of attackers, and for every *shikome* who falls three Tsunu samurai yield up their lives to arrow or to blade.

Issun Boshi urges the *kirin* ahead and commands the beast to descend farther toward the battle. The sounds rise stronger and more clearly; Kishimo can see the faces and armor of the warriors. She recognizes the *kabuto* of Ibaraki with its three peacock feathers at its crest; the helmet of Aizen with its dragon glittering and writhing in the firelight.

The sound of the battle falls away, lower and lower, as ever fewer defenders remain to face the streaming *shikome* horde.

In this battle there is neither retreat nor surrender; two lines of soldiers, Tsunu samurai and invading *shikome,* confront each other. Flights of arrows arc through chilling evening air. Despite the gathering darkness the armies are visible to each other in the flaring light of bonfires dotting the beach. Flights of arrows, and the wounded and the dead fall to earth. Many arrows miss their marks and fall where chance directs: clattering off black jagged rock, slithering in white grainy sand, splashing into hissing, foaming surf.

Those that strike *kabuto, do-maru, kote* armored sleeve, *suneate* leg armor, *kogake* foot armor, *mempo* or *hoate* face masks—all of these clank and clatter, fall to the ground; a few snag in silk armor bindings and warriors snatch at them, place them in their own *ebira,* quivers, to use again.

But here and there an arrow strikes between cuirass and leg armor, between sleeve and body armor, and a warrior falls, bleeding.

Here an arrow aimed with consummate skill—or guided by mocking fortune—passes straight through eye opening of *hoate* metal mask, penetrates a warrior's eye and brain, and causes death before the victim even reaches ground.

Forces advance, arrows cease to fly and instead spears are hurled like javelins, polished blades flashing and lacquered shafts gleaming red and yellow in the light of bonfires.

Again, some miss their targets and fall harmlessly on black rock, white sand, foaming surf. Others, deflected by helmet or shield or armor, fall harmlessly also.

But those that fly with sufficient force penetrate armor at vulnerable points and many bodies fall to earth, red blood pulsing in red firelight, armor stained with pouring lifeblood and crusted with white sand. Here a warrior lies on his side, a long *naga-suyari*-bladed spear passed all through his body, blood running down its lacquered shaft to sand before the warrior, the red-stained blade exposed behind his back.

Here a warrior lies on his back, *jumonji-yari* cruciform spear in his throat, its decorated haft rising straight above him like a *sashimono* battle flag. Slowly the weight of the *jumonji-yari* tilts to one side and the head of the warrior turns like that of a living man until it faces the sea, unseeing eyes peering futilely toward the horizon in search of arriving reinforcements.

Strangely, could he but see, the dead warrior would indeed make note of a ship's arrival.

It is *Ofuna*.

Still observing from overhead are Kishimo, Issun Boshi, Okinu-nushi in the war chariot drawn by the fiery *kirin*. As the final defending samurai falls before the attack of Aizen-myu and the *shikome* of Ibaraki, the bow of *Ofuna* slides onto white sand. The draft of the ship is not great; its hull is flat; the ship, hard-driven by wind elementals commanded by Okinu-nushi, comes to a firm footing on the sand.

Sailors leap from the deck of *Ofuna,* hastening to form in battle ranks and confront the victorious but disorganized *shikome*.

Issun Boshi commands the fiery *kirin* to charge downward and the beast obediently brings the chariot to rest on the shore near the ranks of landing sailors. At the same moment, Ibaraki, shouting urgent commands to his followers, draws them into ranks facing the sailors of *Ofuna*.

The war chariot disgorges its three occupants, even Okinu-nushi, the tallest of the three, standing no higher than the *kogake* foot armor of a nearby sailor-warrior but recently debarked from *Ofuna;* the sailor stares pop-eyed at the three figures and the tiny *kirin*-drawn chariot.

Issun Boshi passes his hands before Okinu-nushi and Kishimo. A crackling sound fills the ears of Kishimo and a feeling of strange energy pervades her body. She grows, as do Okinu-nushi and Issun Boshi. This time, also, the chariot itself and the fiery dragon-horse swell to a size proportionate to the personages all about.

Before Issun Boshi or the others make any further move, the two armies on the beach draw up and mount weapons toward each other, the force of *shikome* acting under the command of the demon king Ibaraki; that of *Ofuna's* erstwhile seamen, under command of their own ship's officers. The *shikome* army, but recently attackers against the defending troops of Tsunu, are now themselves cast in the role of defenders. The sailor-warriors of *Ofuna* are now the attackers.

Where moments before a pitched battle took place between *shikome* and Tsunu, now the *Ofuna* crewmen and surviving *shikome* oppose each other with arrow, spear, sword, and dirk.

The bonfires flicker yet, crackling and hissing, hurling bright sparks and curling columns of smoke into the night air.

But a single figure strides through the teeming armies, ignoring arrow and spear cast, shoving *tachi* and *tanto* and *aikuchi* blades aside as if they were twigs in an undergrown wood through which his strides carry him. He crosses the beach purposefully, drawing to a halt before the trio of Issun Boshi, Okinu-nushi, Kishimo.

He is the man-god Aizen-myu.

Issun Boshi bows courteously to the Aizen. The beach is cleared of our mutual foes, Issun Boshi declares.

Aizen-myu bows in return. Little One Inch, he says, why do you speak of our mutual foes?

Issun Boshi chuckles. Do you not know me, Lord Aizen?

Aizen-myu bends low to peer into the face of the other, for Issun Boshi, Little One Inch, stands no taller at his full stature than did the infant Miroku in his cabin aboard *Ofuna*. Rising again, Aizen shakes his head. I know you are Issun Boshi. How else do I know you, Little Lord One Inch?

Again Issun Boshi laughs. I was the Miroku, he declares. The time has arrived at last for me to come into my own, and for us to settle our differences. For here we are at last in the land of Tsunu, and tomorrow only one of us may rule here.

Aizen-myu nods gravely. You, Issun Boshi, are the Miroku.

Issun Boshi bows. I *was* the Miroku. And now I shall become the champion and the ruler of the land of Tsunu.

Aizen gestures toward the struggling warriors, *shikome* and sailors, whose arms yet clash against each other. The circle of the four—Aizen-myu, Issun Boshi, Okinu-nushi, Kishimo—is surrounded by a zone of safety and quiet. Beyond this zone, men and monsters swing weapons at one another, strike, pierce armor and flesh, scream and fall and bleed and die. Within the circle: only conversation.

How will this battle end? Kishimo asks innocently.

I have only slight powers of prescience, my Lady Kishimo, Aizen-myu responds. Yet I see the outcome here. Death to all.

All? Kishimo repeats questioningly, aghast.

All, Aizen-myu nods. Such is the end of the battle when the armies are too finely balanced. Neither will withdraw. Neither will yield. Each will struggle against the other, on and on, until the final two warriors fall together, mortally wounded. Let us watch!

And the four do so, gazing as if frozen by cold more intense than that of the Forest of Ice and wind-whipped by gales more terrible than those that rally the Sea of Mists into hissing brine.

The battle is not unlike that of the *shikome* horde against the former defenders of Tsunu: arrows, spears, long- and shortswords. Wounds and death. Black rocks spattered with red gore and white sand lined with dark bodies.

But this difference: this time, neither army shrinks through the wounding and death of soldiers. The sailor-warriors of *Ofuna* have long departed their ship in their great numbers, yet the flat-hulled craft remains solidly beached, and a stream of reinforcements trickles slowly from its decks. Sailor-warriors fall and die on the cold sands, and the din and flow of battle passes them by. Replacements, their iron-plate armor, wooden bows, *naginata* lances, and *horimono*-engraved swords fresh, silently slip over the railing from the deck of *Ofuna* and enter the fray, replacing dead comrades.

Demon-samurai *shikome* meet the sailors and engage them, weapon for weapon, thrust for thrust, wound for wound. And as the *Ofuna* warriors fall before the blades of *shikome*, just so do the gnarled creatures fall before the blows and thrusts of the sailors: armor pierced, blood spilled, flesh slashed. *Shikome* lie dying and dead, their bodies mixed uncaring with those of their enemies, slayer and slain sharing brotherly communion in death. And from among the tall black rocks that jut from the sand and define the limits of the beach, replacements for fallen *shikome* stride silently to replace their dead and join the battle.

All the while do uncounted multitudes of *heike* crabs, each with the scowling countenance of an ancient warrior graven on its shell, scuttle from the foamy sea onto the beach, dragging off the bodies of dead warriors, *shikome* monster and *Ofuna* crewman alike, disappearing with them into the black foaming brine, perhaps to bear them to the court of Ryujin the Dragon King of Yomi.

How long will this struggle endure? Kishimo asks Aizen-myu.

The man-god responds: I see no ending to this.

And yet they stand and watch, the four within the circle inviolate, and the battle continues, *shikome* versus *Ofuna*, demon-soldier against sailor-warrior, arrow and blade against shield and helmet and cuirass. The wounded fall and die. *Heike* bear them away and unending streams of new warriors replace them.

At last a faint gray light rises from far beyond the field of battle, and in its pale beams the toiling armies grow not more bright and visible, but themselves faint and translucent. The gray develops a pinkish tinge, then red-orange as the eastern skies grow vivid. Simultaneously the sounds of battle grow softer and the turmoil of killing less substantial.

Now a gleaming chord segment of the Mirror of Amaterasu erupts from behind black rocks, the sky snaps to its daytime brilliance, and the sun pours gleaming brightness upon the beach, the struggle, the observers, and the ship *Ofuna* equally, and in those quick moments of brightness the two struggling armies grow faint, thin, silent before the eyes and ears of the four observers. The *heike* crabs that had covered much of the beach with their scurrying walk and clacking pincers scuttle rapidly back to the sea and disappear beneath its waters.

The ship *Ofuna,* without visible crew, backs from the strand and fades slowly into the morning mist of the sea.

And the Aizen-myu faces Issun Boshi, Kishimo, Okinu-nushi. Only we remain, the man-god intones. We must settle our affairs among ourselves.

The others nod assent.

16

Okinu-nushi the Spirit Master swells and rises, growing slowly
above the others. The contrast is all the greater as the dark
Master stands beside little Issun Boshi, Okinu-nushi towers
above the others, and as he grows taller and broader his
substance is divided and spread ever more thinly. Soon there is
a faint suggestion of sunlight penetrating his body; soon Kishimo
is able to see rocks and brine foam through the dark Master.

Raising his hands in their gesture of power, Okinu-nushi
speaks, his voice still clear although reverberating from a greater
distance than it ever has before.

Farewell, the Spirit Master calls, farewell Issun Boshi once
Lord Miroku. Your transformation leaves you to find your fate
as you will. You have no more need for me; nor I, interest in
you. Farewell to Aizen-myu. Settle your affairs with the others
as you will. You never had need of me and when I sought to
aid you I won mockery from your servant and crony the
shikome Ibaraki. Farewell. Farewell to my Lady Kishimo, you
who grew from weakness and trembling to courage and
strength. You who recieved the sword Kuzanagi have no need
of my little power.

Farewell to all!

The Spirit Master grows taller, broader, ever less dense. His
being is dispersed rather than destroyed, becoming more and
more diffuse, thinner, taller, thinner, broader, until his being
surrounds the others with a flimsy veil that in turn grows still

thinner until its very presence slips beyond the level of perception and is at last gone . . . but not gone: rather, spread so thin that its presence can no longer be seen but may, perhaps, still be felt.

Kishimo releases a deeply held breath; all unknowing, she has stood tense and breathless through the speech and growth and final disappearance of Okinu-nushi. He is truly gone, Kishimo says to the others, truly gone and yet more truly present than earlier.

You think he will never return? Issun Boshi asks. You think that the personage of Okinu-nushi has sped forever from our ken?

Neither Kishimo nor Aizen-myu can answer this question, and there falls upon them, upon the beach of Tsunu where they stand, a deep silence in which the small sounds of foaming sea, tossing breeze, chirping insect, and clacking crab—not the warrior-faced *heike* but simple and humble little shore crabs—rise and fill their ears.

At length Issun Boshi speaks once more. Aizen-myu, he calls, Aizen-myu, the defenders of Tsunu are destroyed, my warriors shall return from *Ofuna* with the fall of another night, and their battle with your *shikome* henchmen resume. The armies will fight for all time, *Ofuna* beaching, sailor-warriors tumbling from her deck to meet teeming *shikome* led by your vassal Ibaraki. Warfare and death forever. The *heike* crabs of this place carrying away the dead to the land of Yomi, to return another night and die once more.

Aizen-myu nods, speaks: Yes, my Lord One Inch, this is the end of our ambitions, those of the Miroku and those of Aizen-myu. Warfare by the flickering flames of bonfires each night and court ceremonies in the palace of Ryujin by day. Forever. A splendid fate for these warriors.

Issun Boshi says: Aizen, would not Ibaraki and all the *shikome* rather proceed in their search for Onogoro?

Aizen moves his head from side to side, holds a hand with its palm downward and gestures his negative. I left the higher realm and entered this one, Aizen-myu says, in search of enlightenment. Perhaps I have gathered some shred of wisdom, my Lord One Inch. I do not claim to have achieved enlightenment, nor do I think an enlightened one would be aware of his state, for such knowledge would carry with it pride, the foe of enlightenment.

Sutras, Lord Aizen? Issun Boshi asks, smiling.

But I believe this, my Lord One Inch, Aizen-myu continues: that the path of existence is of worth and the proper existence is the source of merit. To reach an end is meaningless, for if that end is a final changeless state then the journey has no meaning, for it is a journey to nowhere, and if that end is not nothingness but a new beginning then the journey is also without meaning, for the whole march is but the traversing of a circle and all points of a circle are equally meritorious.

But I believe this, my Lord One Inch: one may tread that path with courage and with kindness and strength, may observe the beauties of the forest that lines the path. For these warriors, *shikome* monsters and *Ofuna's* sailors alike, the nights of battle and days at court may last as long as they will, and the warriors will tread a path that is of worth and of merit for them. While to find the land of Onogoro would be an ending rather than a journey, and hence would be without meaning.

Issun Boshi, Little One Inch, giggles. Well, be it so, he says to Aizen-myu. And what becomes of us, Lord Aizen?

Little One Inch gestures with his perfect miniature hands, the gesture including Kishimo and Aizen-myu as well as himself.

Aizen-myu says: Should we not consult the Lady Kishimo? Her wishes as well as our own must receive consideration.

Issun Boshi bows before the Aizen. You are right, surely. Let us consult the lady.

He turns toward Kishimo and bows once more, a figure like that of a festival doll, perfect in every detail, exquisite and alive. My Lady Kishimo.

Kishimo responds in like manner. Lord One Inch.

Your wish, Lady?

A frown marks Kishimo's face. Although I alone of the three of us am a mortal woman, none of us has the proper parentage or history of the true human. You, my Lord One Inch, are twice born, once to parents as the child Miroku and once to Miroku who was transformed to Issun Boshi the man without growing tall. And my Lord Aizen, a godling who became also a man in order to visit the lower realms in search of enlightenment. While I myself came from some other realm where I was—not man nor woman but both, before becoming woman as Kishimo.

I think this realm has little to offer any of us. My wish, Lord Issun Boshi—or more properly, my thought, my judgment—is that we can only go onward, to whatever place or realm the powers that guide us may choose.

After this Kishimo is silent.

The Aizen-myu bends and holds forth one hand before Issun Boshi, who hops upon it with a laugh.

Wisdom, nods Issun Boshi.

From the mouth of woman, nods Aizen-myu.

How, then, shall such powers be consulted? Kishimo stands facing directly into the Mirror of Amaterasu. From its lacquered scabbard passed beneath her *obi* and fastened to her *do-maru* she draws the sword Kuzanagi and holds it aloft in both her hands. Its bright glimmering is increased by the brilliance of morning: Kuzanagi becomes a mirror of the Mirror; a shimmering, glittering sunlet rolls up and down the *horimono*-etched blade with any slightest movement of Kishimo's arms or hands.

The sword tugs forward and Kishimo marches, holding it like a standard, Aizen-myu close beside her, Issun Boshi riding upon the man-god's *kote* iron sleeve armor like a child carried by its father. With each stride Kishimo's feet make a small hissing sound as they slide upon the pure sand, its whiteness restored with the rising of the sun and the disappearance of the warring armies; even the spilled blood of sailors and *shikome* and Tsunu people is gone.

Kishimo approaches the greatest and harshest of the black granite boulders that rise from the sand and circles it carefully while Kuzanagi's brightness illumines every crevice and cranny; at last the sword, seemingly satisfied, ceases to tug forward and

Kishimo halts, her back to the Mirror of Amaterasu, her shadow cast sharp and doubly black against the black granite.

She raises the sword Kuzanagi high over her head and slashes downward, splitting her own shadow from *kabuto* to *kogake*, from iron helmet with thunderbolt crest to armored feet. The rock opens. Kishimo strides forward, not pausing to study what lies before her nor turning to assure herself that Aizen-myu and Issun Boshi continue in her wake.

For an instant Kishimo is totally disoriented: all light ceases, even that of Kuzanagi; *above* and *below* lose their meaning; the soft mutterings of surf and wind are lost in utter silence. Then Kishimo finds her footing. Kuzanagi blazes alight once more. Kishimo feels the brush of shoulder upon her shoulder and by the light of Kuzanagi's mirror-blade she sees Aizen and One Inch beside her.

But there is nothing beside the three. Their feet rest, however solidly, upon apparent nothingness. There is no light other than that of Kuzanagi's bright blade. There is no sound other than that of their own breathing. There is no color, no substance, nothing beyond themselves.

The sword, still held with its blade upright before Kishimo, tugs forward and upward. Kishimo cries urgently to Aizen-myu the man-god; Issun Boshi, clinging to *kote*, seizes Kishimo's arm in time to be borne aloft with her as the sword Kuzanagi draws her from the place. Her long hair is whipped from beneath its *eboshi* binding cloth and falls behind her, streaming from beneath the neck guard of her *kabuto*. The tips of her hair snap against her armored back, making little tapping sounds that are the only ones heard within the darkness.

They rise, Kishimo, Aizen-myu, Issun Boshi, through the darkness and vacancy. At last they emerge into another region, another realm of lightness. Once more a sun burns overhead but neither its color nor its size is the same as the Mirror of Amaterasu. The air is heavy and moist. The day is warm and rests upon their shoulders like a bundle of straw on the shoulders of a laborer.

Great beasts roar and tower above the three, at first hardly noticing their presence. At last a monster face looms lower before them, scaly lips are drawn back, revealing rows of huge fangs. A long, dark-toned tongue flashes out and back. Tiny bright eyes blink at the three With an awesome scream the great head darts forward; a single move is possible for Kishimo: she strikes with sword Kuzanagi in a great, sweeping upward lunge.

The terrible lizard head is cleft from jaw to nostril. Kishimo hears only the beginning of its terrible roar before she tumbles into the new opening in the fabric of being, drawn once again by the force of Kuzanagi. Again light and color, sound and form, are lost. Again Kishimo, Aizen, Issun Boshi careen through limbo, drawn with breakneck speed by the shining blade. Again they emerge into a new realm: dazzling color here, rainbow shades racing one after another to color an amorphic surrounding.

Whirling, tumbling, spinning dizzily, they fetch up at last in the midst of a grassy meadow where humming insects rise in late afternoon warmth and laziness. A brook purls nearby. Birds float lazily overhead. Small animals scuttle through tall grasses and underbrush.

Kishimo turns in a full circle, sees no threat, sheathes her shining sword. Silhouetted on the near horizon is a tall structure. Pagoda-like in form, as grand and splendid as a palace, the building shines in lowering sunlight. Kishimo and her companions begin a steady walk toward the building. Before they have covered half the distance, a figure rises from a high balcony and soars toward them: a wizened grandfather mounted upon a flaming bird, a long-legged, rose-colored flamingo. The slim bird and its rider beat through the sky and circle over the heads of the three travelers, slowly descending toward them.

The flamingo drops to earth and the ancient figure dismounts with the slow care of his years. He approaches the travelers and bows courteously. Kishimo, Aizen-myu, Issun Boshi also bow to the old one.

The ancient man raises his head and, smiling, snatches Little

One Inch from the arm of Aizen. With disarming speed he peels the armor from Issun Boshi and pops the miniature man into his mouth, revealing rows of long yellow fangs.

Kishimo sweeps Kuzanagi from its scabbard even as the old man swallows Little One Inch. In an instant Issun Boshi reaches the stomach of the old man and the ancient's robes dance and heave with the struggles of Issun Boshi inside his belly. Kishimo swings Kuzanagi, slicing the robe of the old man, opening his belly like Susano-wu opening the body of the eight-headed serpent, and like the babies of Izumo pouring forth from the belly of the serpent, Issun Boshi leaps whole and unharmed from the carcass of the ancient man.

Issun Boshi leaps into the purling stream, cleanses himself of the smirchment of the old man's innards and again dons his armor, then bows before Kishimo, thanking her for his rescue.

The old man, meanwhile, dances and shouts angrily at Kishimo. You have ruined my finest gown, the ancient complains. And you have robbed me of my meal! This is my domain and I am entitled to feast on the beasts of my own fields. Now I must hasten home and sew up my poor belly and my ruined gown. You will hear from me, I will not forget this affront!

The old man leaps upon the back of his flamingo, which flaps into the air, carrying him away, returning to the tall pagoda from which it has brought him.

Kishimo strides quickly to the purling stream and wades in it to a large gray rock. She smites the rock with Kuzanagi and follows the sword into the opening, accompanied by Aizen-myu and Issun Boshi. They fall through the familiar blackness and feel the usual sense of vertigo, then soar behind Kuzanagi and emerge into a strange cloudy realm where creatures of shimmering ice duel with beings of yellow-red flame.

All are armed with sword and lance, and while armies face each other, pairs of warriors duel evenly matched, a being of ice and a being of flame, the frigid warrior attacking with glittering blue-white lance, icicles hanging from *kabuto,* frost condensing from mouth; the warrior of flame defending with a shield of dancing fire, gold, red, blue, his breath glowing, his hair leaping upward in flame.

Aizen-myu sets a spirit-wall of gray translucence between the travelers and this great battle; through its protection they observe for a time, then Kishimo rends the spirit-wall with the glittering blade and they stride through the rent, not into the battle of ice and flame but into another realm where it is dawn and tribes of hairy half-men clash with club and fang, screaming defiance at one another, dancing up and down with rage, pounding their chests with gnarled fists and the dry earth with heavy clubs, then charge, darting in and out, delivering a blow with a heavy wooden club or seizing an opponent with talon-like claws and ripping at exposed tender parts, gouging eyes, tearing away genitals.

As if a gong had sounded to bring a signal, the half-men freeze suddenly in their tracks, then turn as one toward Kishimo, Aizen-myu, Issun Boshi. An army of throats roar at once and hairy creatures begin a growling, slouching advance toward the three. Aizen-myu raises his hands to summon a spirit defense once again but Kishimo halts him, opens the very earth with Kuzanagi, and they plunge once more into the void, to emerge in the center of a terrible storm.

They are standing in the midst of a veld-like plain, tall grasses and low shrubbery stretching far in all directions. The sky is filled with black clouds, and thunderbolts flash from billowing head to billowing head, from cloud to earth all about them. With a final shattering detonation the storm breaks and the very earth shakes beneath the impact of the torrent.

The falling drops are warm, heavy, smashing down upon the helmets and armored shoulders of the three. Within brief moments the water begins to accumulate on the hard, dry earth; despite the grass and shrubbery the earth is packed solidly here and it cannot absorb the rain as it falls.

Gray-brown streams spring into being. Puddles appear, grow into ponds before the eyes of the travelers, then into small lakes. Amphibious creatures, lying low in summer aestivation among the grasses and shrubs, stir into life, at first sluggishly, then with quickening vigor. A silver-scaled serpent writhes between the feet of Kishimo and disappears into darkling grasses. A reptile the size of a house cat perches in the branches of a stiff-twigged bush and snaps at passing batrachians.

Thunderbolts continue to play about the heavens and to crash from the storm above to the water-running plain.

The accumulating waters begin to roll across the plain, its canted surface turning it now into a gigantic river leagues in width. The grasses are submerged, small bushes dragged from the earth and swept past Kishimo, Aizen-myu, and tiny Issun Boshi, who clings tightly to the armored sleeve and cuirass of the Aizen.

A mighty thunderbolt falls from the heavens, crashing upon the branches of a tall, broad bush and setting it aflame. Across the dark-faced river, the bush flares like a giant's beacon torch, smoking and hissing but maintaining its flame and heat against the beating downpour, a single red-yellow blob on the face of the dark water beneath the now black sky.

Alarmed at the crashing bolts, Kishimo holds the sword Kuzanagi overhead, the flaring brilliance of its blade outshining the flames of the burning shrub. With a grumble and a jolt the blackest of the storm clouds unleashes a giant thunderbolt, yellow-green, jagged, sizzling and jouncing from cloud to cloud, from cloud to earth, from earth back to heaven, finally tumbling its jagged way through the rain-streaked sky to the fist and thunderbolt of metal stylized and standing upright on Kishimo's own helmet, *nigiryu no kabuto.*

Kishimo feels the terrifying energy of the thunderbolt flaring downward from the crest of her helmet, flooding all her body with its brilliance and energy, turning her very bones and meat into a streaming beacon that illuminates the whole plain and river as brightly as the sun, dazzling Aizen-myu and Issun Boshi, then gathering and flooding upward, from legs and crotch and belly into her chest, her arms, and into the blade Kuzanagi, whose dazzling brilliance is doubled and trebled and doubled again.

The sword dances in Kishimo's hands like a living thing, drawing her with it, whipping her feet from the deepening flood, leaving the man-god Aizen-myu and the Little Lord One Inch to find their own destiny beyond the storm.

Kishimo rises, rises behind Kuzanagi, to the teeming storm clouds, plunges into their roiling blackness that dances with discharging sparks and tiny thunderbolts, whirling her and buffeting her with cold and wetness, then springs from the upper surface of their storm into a realm of tranquil blue where the Mirror of Amaterasu glares downward and the sword Kuzanagi's brilliance is suddenly withdrawn, not fading or failing but simply returning to the blade itself, where deep-etched *horimono* once more become discernible and the dancing energies of the blade ripple up and down its length in slowly diminishing agitation.

Panting, exhausted, Kishimo lowers the sword, slides it carefully back into its scabbard, drops her hands to her sides, and gazes about, trying to reorient herself after her whirling transit through the myriad realms.

She drops to lotus position, doffs her *nigiryu no kabuto* and armor. A gentle breeze springs up, warm and moist as the steam from a hot cleansing tub. Kishimo sighs, draws doeskin *yugake* from her hands, looses her *obi* and kimono and headband. She draws the sword Kuzanagi carefully from its scabbard and lays it across her lap, its polished-lacquer handle lying across the crease of hip and thigh, the *horimono*-decorated blade passing across her pelvis, beneath her belly, gleaming in yellow contrast to the black tightness between her legs.

The warmth of the breeze and of the sun relaxes her muscles; she feels the warmth on her graceful bosom, uncovered for the first time since her ice-drenched encounter with Aizen-myu.

The sun spreads its disk across the sky, growing ever greater but no brighter, until Kishimo finds herself in a universe of diffused light and warmth. The brightness grows less, the moisture and the breeze fade away, leaving behind not darkness nor aridity nor even a stillness, but a neutral cosmos into which

Kishimo herself slowly ebbs, not as into death but into a state of total suffusion and peace.

There is not light nor dark, neither heat nor cold, not life nor death. There is, perhaps, a sound of distant, faint music, of soprano horns and snares, the faint hissing of most minuscule particles, and then that too is gone.